I
AM STILL
COMMITTED..

as hopes are yet to die.

I
AM STILL
COMMITTED..

as hopes are yet to die.

Soumitro Chatterjee

Srishti
PUBLISHERS & DISTRIBUTORS

Srishti Publishers & Distributors
N-16, C. R. Park
New Delhi 110 019
srishtipublishers@gmail.com

First published by
Srishti Publishers & Distributors in 2012
2nd impression 2012

Copyright © Soumitro Chatterjee 2012

Typeset by EGP at Srishti

In the hope that someday, somewhere
you may read this too…………

Acknowledgement

ﾱ

As this is my debut novel, I have a long list of people whom I want to thank and without them this effort of mine would have remained in my diary.

First of all, I would like to thank the girl without whom I could never have thought of dreaming high in every field I walk now. Some children are born lucky- it's applicable to me for the continuous support and encouragement I got from my Dad, Mom, Brother (Subir Chatterjee) and Sister (Suparna Chatterjee). A big thanks to my best friend Prakash, my roomies, all friends during engineering life, all colleagues of my company and friends who have motivated me in some way or the other.

My special thanks to Shilpi Dutta, Smriti Parashar, Gagan Paji, Shruti Didi, Hiten Sahai Bahri and Rahul Bagchi whose editorial contribution cannot be measured. I thank the whole Srishti team who has shown confidence in me and given me the opportunity to turn my dream into reality.

I would like to extend my gratitude to my Dean-placement, principal and all faculty members of my Engineering College. Credit goes to the kids of Prayas who have been my source of inspiration from the day I became a part of their lives.

Last but not the least, I thank my readers who spent time to look into my life, as without you, my book would have been lying on the rack from where you decided to pick it up.

Before you start.......

౭౩

Dear Readers, many of you might be curious to know what made me write this book. But before that, let me tell you something; during my engineering life in Chennai when I used to see novels in the market, based on true stories, I had a strong feeling that writers wanted to sell their stories for a small amount by quoting them as true stories. But I realized the fact behind it only when I started writing.

It's not always that you find people around you to listen to you. At times even if you have people around you, some circumstances or responsibilities make it imperative to keep your things to yourself, and exactly at that time a pen and an old diary becomes an important part of your life. I don't claim to be extraordinary in writing, however I want to convey that many of you who feel that your memories of life can be cherished forever, losing anything is the end and there is no-one to help or hear you out, just pick up a pen and paper and start writing. If it clicks and becomes your passion which pushes you to go extra miles, you too can end up writing something worthwhile.

This is exactly how I started. Many pages were wasted and many diaries were filled but with all the support of the people around me, I could present my work in front of you. Though writing my debut novel has no specific reasons as such, yet I wanted to share many things which were in my heart since long. This is how my journey of writing started.

Your feedback/suggestions are valuable for me.

www.soumitrochatterjee.com
Mail me @ chatterjee.soumitro87@gmail.com

Where It Begins....

℃

I t was not the first time in my life that I felt something strong for some girl. I remember the time when I was in standard first, while going to school with that girl in rickshaw, sitting on her lap and switching places in turns, made me think it was love- my first love.

However, that thought didn't glue to me for long and was proved wrong when as a student of standard sixth, while eating *samosa* and playing *kho-kho* daily with her (a new one), I discovered my love in her.

Priya proved me wrong. It was she, whom I thought was my true love; that cracking the IIT entrance would be a stepping stone to win her.

I left my home town (Dhanbad the coal-capital of India and a small city on the map of India, which provides the second highest revenue to Indian Railway after Mumbai) for Delhi, the national capital. I spent one year at a premier Institute in Delhi for my preparation and from that time till now, I have been asking myself, "What is love?" I have always heard people saying that true love happens only once in a life. I wonder, "Who were those characters in my life, if they were not my love."

Getting into an IIT remained a dream and I moved out of Delhi to join an Engineering College in Chennai. I still l believe, it was one of the few right decisions I have taken so far; rest all were taken by my parents and siblings since I am the youngest in my family.

Chennai- a city which I didn't like in the initial days but later it became the place which taught and blessed me with so many things, that today I cannot neglect its importance whenever I look at myself. I had been in Chennai earlier during December 1998, when I had represented my state in All India National Children Science Congress Contest. I had stayed at Anna University during that tenure. But there was a huge difference between that experience and this one, since last time it was a stay of mere five days while later it was meant to be a four year long journey.

I still remember the date and time. It was 20th August 2005, around 4:30 am. A black trunk with my name painted in white "Soumitro Chatterjee" besides my Dad and I, stood facing the entrance of Chennai Central Railway Station. My Dad asked me to wait there till he inquired about a hotel nearby. I heard a group of boys talking amongst themselves about a college.

Since I am good in interacting with people, I mingled with the group and found them going to the same college where I was. All of them hailed from district Bihar and having found people from the same place, it made me happier. It was a group of seven and then including me, we were eight in number.

My Dad returned from the inquiry counter and was surprised to see seven heads greeting him with a "Hello." I told him that they would join the same college and asked my Dad to book a hall since we were nine by then. Sumit (the guy who became one of my close buddies later) said –"No, No, we are ten, since my Dad is also here." We decided to book a *Dharamshala* nearby, to spend rest of the day, as we were supposed to report near Pandalai Hospital to board the bus next morning. The day passed by interacting with each other.

The next morning, we were ready quite early since the

college bus was scheduled for arrival at 7:00 am. We reached at the mentioned address much before time. Our college campus was about fifty kilometers away from that point, near the sea shore of Mamallapuram. We all were excited for the journey, as if it was going to be a picnic trip for us. But for some reason unknown, we had to wait for three hours and hence were losing our patience .The number of people waiting there had increased to hundred by that time.

At last, the bus arrived around 10:30 am. We all jumped into it to occupy our seats. Our parents were angry and blamed the college authorities for their mismanagement. The bus was fully packed; in fact more than thirty people were standing. I was on a seat with my gang, adjusting five people on a seat meant for three. Majority of the crowd inside the bus was from Bihar, Jharkhand and West Bengal.

Abruptly, a person announced, "Those who don't have a seat please get down."

I had to de-board the bus. "First bring another bus. Then only we will get down," I protested. Who knew we might have to wait for another three hours!

"Don't shout!" that dumb looking person snarled at me.

"You don't shout," responded my father angrily.

That boorish conversation was enough to ignite fire among us —"*Maaro sale ko maaro*" (beat the hell out of him), shouted everyone in the bus. He had no other option other than taking an exit from the bus.

After the high pitch drama, the bus took off with the number of people equaling the number of seats, followed by another bus. We were laughing, discussing that they might have understood the fire in us (Biharis), as rightly said by Abhinav, one of the member of our gang.

The scenery was stunning, while crossing ECR (East Coast Road). On one side of the road, there was the beautiful sea and the other side of the road was complimented by coconut trees in a row. The fun filled journey began as we started singing and shouting, in spite of the repeated objections by the conductor. There were few girls with us in the bus, but none of us interacted with them since it was the time to build the guys gang.

After an hour, the bus entered the campus main gate.

"Oooooo!" hooted everyone and I followed it.

It was Kalpana Chawla block where the bus stopped and we correctly guessed it as the girl's hostel, since within few seconds we saw girls getting out of the bus. Again, I don't know why, we hooted, as we knew that it was going to be the centre of attraction for us in the coming years.

The bus resumed its journey and we started the recently invented rhythmic tone "Ooooo!" Our parents, who were seated in the front of the bus, whenever turned around, we acted as if nothing had happened and we were the most innocent children in this world!

It was boy's hostel now, the C.V.Raman block at last, where the bus stopped. We took our luggage. The warden instructed us to make a queue so that he could allocate rooms to us. There was an uneasy shuffle amongst us, as everyone tried to change the position to get a roommate of their choice, but we eight did not move.

It was, Abhishek, Prabhat and I who got room number five which became the epicenter of all good and bad things later!

Raj, Sumit and Abhinav were allocated room number six. We wished someone would accompany Jassi and Anil, as only two known faces were left in our group, but perhaps it was almighty's wish to restrict our group size to eight.

"You have an attached bathroom but one shouldn't use that, space is less in your room, so only two boys can take this room" said the warden,

Room numbers five, six and seven were allocated to us and our happiness knew no bounds with this allotment. After all, the gang of eight was together! We settled in before the lunch time. We had lunch with our parents quickly and returned to our rooms.

It was time for our parents to go back to their respective home towns. I was in Delhi for a year, away from my parents, however at that time I was with my elder brother .This was the very first time where I would be alone, some twenty four hundred kilometers away from them!

I grew quite emotional, feeling terrible to bid bye to my Dad who was equally sad to leave his youngest son, so far from him. All eight of us went to drop Sumit's and my Dad to the railway station. Both of them had their train scheduled to Howrah at 11:35pm. We reached the station around 5:00 pm.There was no point in waiting till late night, so our parents asked us to return to the hostel as early as possible as it was a new place for all of us. While on the way to our hostel, I realized it for the first time that I had sacrificed my home, those streets where I used to play and roam around and my best friend Prakash, to get an Engineering degree.

The following day was the first day at college for us; as a result we slept early. Three washrooms, three toilets, twenty four guys in one corridor and everyone had the same reporting time - 9:15 Am. It was a Tom and Jerry race to occupy either of washroom or toilet. Jassi and I planned to exchange washroom and toilet respectively, once we were done with it. I followed the healthier way - first toilet, then washroom for a bath. Jaspal had no alternative left, but to go in the reverse direction! ☺

We all assembled in the auditorium.

The formal meeting started, where our principal, dean, professors and the staff were introduced. Jassi, Abhishek, Raj, Prabhat, Sumit and I were from the same department of Electronics. All were allocated and instructed to go to our respective classes.

The batch of one hundred and twenty students of our department was divided into sections. Jassi and Abhishek got section A, Raj and Prabhat got section B while Sumit and I got section C, all allocated alphabetically.

"Oh nooooo," exclaimed an excited Sumit as we entered our section, room no 31.

"What happened" I asked.

"No girls in our section" replied Sumit making a strange face.

Somehow with all guys, the fun began and those classes followed.

Gradually it became a daily habit - talking about girls in the evening, going for a walk after dinner around girl's hostel, those midnight birthday bumps, and spreading the rumor of a ghost's presence in the hostel. Every other day Jassi used to talk about a girl named Aastha who was very sincere for studies, didn't talk much with anyone, beautiful in looks, stylish and above all had an attitude!

I was called "Dada" by my group members by that time.

One day while discussing about Aastha with Jassi after dinner, I made a remark *"Main to ghaas bhe na dalu us bandi ko."* (I would not even care to talk to her)

I remember, it was September 5th -Teacher's Day. I had gone to buy a gift for a professor, our faculty advisor whom I used to admire a lot. So I went to Kodambakkam to buy the best possible gift for her.

Unexpectedly I received a call from Jassi, "I've told her what you said last night and I have given your number to her."

I didn't get Jassi's point.

I stood scratching my head and in the meantime, I received a text message from an unknown number +91-9884****00 which read, "Can you bring two lemon for me?" I could easily judge who the sender was!

"Why should I?" I replied

A reply followed, the very next moment "*Apni bahan ke liye itna nahi kar sakte?*" (Would you not do this little favor for your sister?)

I got furious. She burnt my self-respect & I got irritated. Instantaneously I decided to settle scores with her one day with a reply, more hurting to her.

Ragging is strictly prohibited in the Campus.

ೞ

Every engineering, medical or degree colleges these days have these words prominently written on big banners during the beginning of the session, "Ragging is strictly prohibited in the Campus." My college was no exception either. Whether such kind of banners have any practical relevance or not but they definitely make freshers think that they can breathe freely in the campus. It was not more than 20 days since our classes had began and we were rigorously following the Nine to Four routine of daily classes.

Freshers like us sheltered themselves or let's say remained hidden in the hostel. Numerically, our batch fairly had outnumbered our seniors but we underestimated the fact "Seniors are always seniors" for which we had to pay heavily. Ragging still was strictly prohibited but only on the banners!

Our group used to be spotted together all the time and we never missed an opportunity to display our unity, whether it was queuing up like ants for having lunch or while moving in the campus, it seemed to others as if we were glued together. Our unity had an exponential enhancement effect on our confidence too and we hardly bothered about being ragged. Our seniors too were totally aware of it.

One day Sumit and I failed to accompany our group on time to the college, as others had to leave early for the workshop. Later, when the two of us were on our way from the hostel to college which barely was a five hundred meters walk, two tall, dark, bulky boys seized our hands and said something in a language which though we didn't understand but seemed Tamil to us. We thought of escaping immediately from that place but in the meantime another senior interrupted and asked us to meet them behind the canteen post lunch.

It was for the first time that we both wanted the lectures not to end by any means and wished that lunch would never happen. At tea break, we joined the others in the group and narrated them our encounter with the seniors. Together we decided that Sumit and I need not go to meet them, and planned to tackle the consequences later. We did not intend it to be a disrespect to our seniors but our point was "Why behind the canteen?" We remained clueless. The same day while returning to our hostel, no body stopped us, nor did any of the seniors come to us. Infact everything carried on in a normal course for a week.

After a week we had to buy some material for our assignment which was not available at our college campus. Though we were aware of many of our seniors living in Kelambakkam and Mahaballipuram yet the urgency of the assignment made it mandatory for us to go to either of these places. Again it was Sumit and I who had to go. Somehow we gathered courage to go to Kelambakkam which was fifteen kilometers away from college. The major reason for choosing Kelambakkam was a comparatively sparse number of seniors residing there.

Finally we boarded bus number 115 from our college and within 30 minutes we reached Kelambakkam. We had already planned that once we get the required things we would return to the hostel. As per our plan, we bought the things in hurry and boarded the bus stand feeling blessed not to have encountered any senior. But destiny had some other plans and we saw the same seniors who had asked us to meet them behind the canteen few days back. Our throats went dry and we felt as if they had been waiting for us. Left with no other alternative, we wished them.

"Good afternoon sirrrrrrr!

I said, - "You know we were about to come that day but my loose motions hindered my way. I had to go the hostel and I took Sumit along with me too."

One among them said, "Ok loose motion? Good, very good."I had no idea about what was so good about loose motion that he appreciated it so many times. He asked if I was still suffering from it.

Thinking that he was concerned about my health, I replied at once, "No sir, I am perfectly ok now."

My answer was enough to trap me in my own knit net. They wanted us to visit their room right then. I tried to avoid the meeting by giving another reason that our friend is not well, we were here to get some medicine but that didn't convince them. Reluctantly we had to follow them.

While trailing them on the way, what felt like an invitation to hell for us, Sumit gave a weird look to me as if it was me who was responsible for this and that at least the rear side of canteen would have been a better option than that? Finally after taking four right and six left turns, we reached a room where around eight seniors welcomed us.

As we entered the room choked with cigarette smoke, within seconds we heard a door slam shut behind us; even the ECG would have shown our heartbeats out of range. We were ridiculed of our heroism which we had displayed by not showing up after they had called us. We silently prayed for the messy situation to end the soonest possible.

And there began our next few hours in hell. We were asked to introduce ourselves. Our voices told it all how much we were scared to speak and the expressions on their face boasted of an accomplishment; the biggest achievement of their life. Out of the blue, one amongst them known as Vijay held my neck and said-

"Hey buddy, don't panic and just chill!"

I thought to myself "Obviously for you people this is time to chill."

Though his moustache and beard did make him resemble like a timid goat, yet his words comforted us for a while. After our introduction, they asked us to clean the utensils which were left unclean in the kitchen sink. Never in my life, I had done this at home and we had to clean a hell lot of utensils in fifteen minutes. It felt as if those idiots had never cleaned their utensils in their entire life. I assumed some of those dirty utensils might have grown fungus on their moist surfaces. Every few minutes, a senior would come and have a look at us as if he was watching the biggest reality show of their lifetime. We were boiling with rage but since we were inside a lion's den, we didn't have any way to escape. Somehow we managed to wash all the utensils.

Mukesh Sir, a senior, offered us two chairs to sit on. We could smell something fishy, lest why should they treat us in a royal way. As I was about to sit, someone got enlightened with an old trick and pulled back my chair. Everybody laughed as I badly hurt my ass.

Suppressing my anger, somehow I got up on my feet. Another senior held Sumit's neck and ordered him to clean the room with the cloth kept below his toe without touching the cloth with hands or legs. It was a tricky thing to do but their stern facial expressions warned that he had to do it there and then. Sumit was in an embarrassing situation and he had to clean the room with his ass. I could do nothing except being a witness to his humiliation.

One fat ass asked me to abuse the rotating fan without repeating any abusive word until the fan stopped rotating after being switched off. If I did repeat, I would have to start all over again with new abuses. It seemed that my new task looked easy to Sumit as he gave a look of confidence to me but for me coming up with new abusing words every time was a bit tough. On one side, Sumit was cleaning the room with his ass and in the other corner of the room I was pacing with the slowing speed of the fan with my words. I don't remember exactly how long it took for the fan to stop but thankfully my seniors did consider dog, pig and other animal names as abusive words.

They continued tormenting us when suddenly one of them, God knows how, struck upon a new idea to play a game with us. Truth Chair – the game was named so and a chair was put in the centre of the room. Of course, we were asked to take the hot seats. I felt as if I was going to sit on an electric chair meant for capital punishment in certain countries. Both of us were too tired and disturbed by then and Sumit's exasperation was visible on his face. We were bombarded with logical and illogical questions. Tears rolled out from our eyes which seemed to be entertaining them like performance during an item number.

It had almost dark outside .All of a sudden, I don't know what made Sumit take such a step; He got up from his chair and in the spur of the moment, ran out of the room and headed towards the terrace. The seniors with me at their footsteps followed him. Till the time I reached the terrace, I heard one senior shout, "Ohhhhhhhhhh noooooooooo."

I was too horrified to figure out what had actually happened. When I reached there, I saw all the seniors standing aghast without Sumit not being visible anywhere. I was petrified and looked around for Sumit but he was nowhere. I screamed at the seniors and fired them with my question "Where is Sumit? Where is my friend?"

I peeped down from the terrace walls, to find bushes all around and a well just besides the boundary wall.

All of us rushed to the ground floor. We crept in near the well but weren't able to trace him in the dark. Did he fall into the well? Or did he run away from there? What exactly happened to him was not known to anyone.

We searched around and suddenly I located Sumit lying unconscious entangled between the bushes. I sprung towards him, calling his name and tried to wake him up. As I touched his head, there was blood all around. I froze for a second.

"Shit" exclaimed one senior. I warned that they all would be dead if anything happened to Sumit.

All seniors were nervous. Much in pain and worry, I hurled abuses at the seniors like anything. Four of the seniors carried Sumit back to the room. His head was bleeding heavily. Two seniors left on their bike to call the doctor and two of them started cleaning the blood. I was crying aloud but all the seniors were too busy nursing Sumit. Within minutes, they cleaned the blood and after bandaging him, made him comfortably sleep on bed. The doctor put two stitches on his head and asked us to bring some medicines on an urgent basis. I was calculating the money left in my wallet when one senior immediately left the room, and within half an hour, returned with the medicines in addition to juice and fruits for Sumit and me.

The way they had treated us few hours earlier and the way they treated us then was entirely different. They were looking after us, as if we were their younger brothers. I was surprised at this sudden transition. I told one of them that our warden would shout if we didn't return on time. He instantly dialed our warden's phone number and told him that we two would stay with them, calling me his younger brother. He passed on the phone to me and something within me forced me say "Yes." After getting my confirmation, warden granted us the permission.

Sumit was getting better and by then the atmosphere of the room had become friendly. About that night, I could only recall the royal service and support we received. We had a fantastic dinner together and even our dishes were cleaned by the seniors. Probably it was Sumit's stream of blood which had changed everything. Next morning Sumit was taken to nearby hospital by the seniors for a CT-scan and none of them left until reports were found to be normal. They were evidently happy and relaxed and so was I.

We all had our breakfast together in a restaurant. Of course the seniors paid for it. We both were fed up of the horrible food in our hostel mess. The lavish breakfast refreshed our taste buds. Finally two seniors rode us back to the college. While they were parking their bikes, we stood there confused, thinking weather we should thank them or point out their mistake. Finally Ravi Sir (one of the seniors) said –"It's now up to you people. The Principal room is just besides you; you can go inside and complain about us. But do take care." They ignited the engines and vanished from the parking lot.

We both looked at each other with blank expression. We started walking. To our right it was the principal room and the left way led to the hostel.

While moving ahead we saw the same banner –"Ragging is strictly prohibited in the campus" .It stood true, because the last night incident did not take place in the campus!

At last we decided to take the left lane, which was right for us and we returned to our hostel.

Hero-Through a Lie….

☙

Room Number. 5; located at the corner of the corridor just beside the washroom, was occupied by Abhishek, Prabhat and me, had three different beds in three corners of the room and the fourth corner was occupied by our used clothes and luggage, a typical Boys' room, I guess !

Evil thoughts kicked my mind every now and then and I was desperately waiting for that one chance of taking revenge from the girl named Aastha. Prabhat was busy in listening to music with his headphone and Abhi was simply lying on bed as usual. I still remember it was somewhere around 3pm, when suddenly Abhi shouted in a loud voice, "Hey I have heard Mahaballipuram is very close by. How about going there now?"

"Now?" shouted Prabhat. "No, we are new to this place and by 6 pm we have to return, so we should not go."

But I looked at Abhishek and he gave me the same mischievous look… Without uttering any other word, we both sprang to our feet and started wearing the least dirty T-shirts and Jeans. Frankly speaking, it was hard to find any, but I managed black jeans and yellow T-shirt and Abhi pulled out a decently clean red shirt paired with a three quarter.

Prabhat was surprised with our sudden preparation and asked us, "Hey where are you guys going at this hour?"

"To see the sea," replied Abhi and we both started for the voyage. Abhi and I, both were pretty excited to enjoy the evening at Mahaballipuram Beach. We took a bus from outside our college campus and exchanged a number of silly thoughts with each other, as spending an evening on a beach was going to be the first ever experience for both of us. We also got to know from other guys in the hostel that there was a *Foreigner's beach*, where lot of *babes* used to take sun bath. We both were literally praying that the sun doesn't set by the time we reach.

Luckily we reached in 35 minutes. As we got down from the bus, I was shocked to see a huge number of foreigners, though it was a shock cum pleasant surprise for me! It seemed as if Abhi and I were the foreigners, as the rest of the population there was not like us. Abhi pushed me and asked me to look out for foreigner's beach, before the sun set. When I inquired from a man about the same, he didn't say anything but pointed his finger opposite to where we were going.

After walking for ten minutes, I again inquired from another person and he asked us to take a left from the first right and then a right from the second left. Ah! That was confusing, but we both were happy to imagine that in the next two minutes, we might get to see many things. After tirelessly walking for three kilometers, we found that we were exactly at the same place from where we had started. The person who had pointed out the way to us with his finger, was not present there, otherwise I would have broken his finger!

Abhishek gave me a weird look and asked me to wait, as it was his turn then to make a query. He went to a shop from where he was not visible to me. After approximately three minutes, he came out of the shop, when I was busy watching the babes passing by me.

"It's really hard to judge the age of these foreigner girls," I said.

Abhi, who had come back with a cigarette in his hand, hit me on my head and said, "Idiot she was not a girl. She was an aunty!"

I was still staring at that girl or aunty, whatever! Does it really matter, especially when the aunty appearing to be a girl is hot!

I saw Abhi walking in the opposite direction to the one where we went last time. I kept asking, "Hey have you asked him properly? Is this the only way to Foreigner's Beach?"

His long steps, because of his height, were almost making me run instead of walking. He didn't reply to my questions and seemed to be busy with his cigarette.

When we reached there and looked ahead, it was a blue colored bed sheet that was spread over a million hectares of land, which was nothing else but the sea. It was not the first time that I was witnessing the beauty of the sea, but that day it looked entirely different. Those waves, that clarity of water made me imagine me as a fish; life would have been so beautiful inside the sea. Unfortunately, I never learnt swimming, but even if I had, I wonder who could have defeated those sky touching tides.

"Oh my God!" shouted Abhishek. "Hey, let's follow her."

I was confused, whom to follow and where to go?

"Don't speak you fool, just follow me," said Abhi and I started following him.

We were on foreigner's beach; I realized when I saw those beautiful girls in small dresses. It was unusual for Abhi and me, but for them it was normal.

"Hey, let's take a picture or a video of this and we will show Prabhat what he has missed," I said.

As I was about to do that, I heard the sound of a whistle approaching us.

"What is this bullshit??" I asked Abhi.

"You cannot stand on this beach, either you leave this place or keep walking," said a fatty uncle to us. I thought he saw me taking pictures and would snatch the camera from us, the way it used to happen in our college.

"Leave this place- so early? It's impossible!" We both said the same thing to each other and then we started walking.

There were so many hot girls around that we both were confused, whom to see and whom to give a miss!

Pointing to a girl, Abhi said, "That girl resembles the one who was in the porn movie we watched last night!!"

We both laughed and kept on walking. Abhi was through with his cigarette. Suddenly we saw a girl standing alone on the beach.

"Let's go there and speak to her, lets see if something works out," I told Abhi. And this time Abhi followed me, as he was well aware that it would be me who would interact with the girl. As we went there, we both kept a little distance away from the place where she was standing. I stood thinking how to initiate, as I had no prior experience of beginning a conversation with a foreigner.

Luckily, a thought came to my mind and I started throwing water on Abhishek. I was sure that if I did that, Abhi would do the same. The girl was standing next to me and as Abhi threw water on me, I bent down a bit. The water splashed straight away to that girl. She got drenched and I got my way to start the conversation.

"Hey, I'm so sorry!"

"It's Ok," said that girl in a sweet voice. I wanted to hear something more from her, but she said the same thing again.

I took the conversation ahead.

"It seems you are upset today." As I said this to her, she looked at me and took a step closer to me.

"Not exactly but……"

"But?" I asked.

She said, "But I am a bit worried as my sister back in Germany is not well...."

"Oh! I am so sorry for her. Is she fine?" and blaah blaah blahh, we continued the conversation.

As Abhi was not so good in interacting with strangers, he made himself comfortable at a boat nearby, which was tied at the sea-shore. Whenever I looked at him, he gave me look which was well understood. He was extremely jealous of me and in the meanwhile we were busy exchanging thoughts on various topics like why she was in India, how about Germany and so on..

I thought Abhi might feel bored since it was more than thirty minutes since we were talking. I called Abhishek and introduced him to her.

"Meet my friend Abhishek and Abhishek this is Carron." The first word from Carron made Abhishek very happy and which was – "Nice name Abhishek."

Then, it was Carron, Abhishek and me, talking to each other, as if we had been friends for a long time. By then it was almost 5:30pm and the sun was about to set. We found Carron playing with water at that time. Who wanted to miss that opportunity? Both of us joined the party and it was like rain dance for us. Within five to ten minutes, we all were drenched from top to bottom and Carron was smiling and laughing out loud. I could see the relaxation on her face. As she had come alone to India for some Research on Indian Culture, she might have felt lonely and who doesn't like to have a company, especially when you are sad.

She was enjoying the moment and so were Abhi and I. She was not more than 23 years old, but the way she was carrying herself was very elegant. I was looking at her, suddenly something flashed in my mind, "Is this what we call love?" I silently laughed a lot and reminded myself of the resolution I made when I had joined engineering college.

Suddenly, her next statement made both Abhi and me silent for a moment.

"Hey you guys come down to my hotel and get yourselves to dry. Then we would have food and drinks together." Several thoughts started running in our minds, but I don't know what made me reply, quite loudly, "Nooooo, we are fine and it is getting late as we have to return to our hostel."

I don't know, was it with my reply or the pitch and tone I used, she looked bit hurt and said, "If you guys don't mind, can I have a picture with you?"

Our happiness was many folds to hear that and then followed the photo session. Abhi with her, me with her, Abhi and me; all possible permutations and combinations! I thought that photo session was over but then suddenly Abhi said, "Can I have your picture in my cell?" So, once more, began the permutation and combination; me with her, Abhi with her; until Abhi took enough pictures of her, from every possible angle.

At last she bid us goodbye and left for her hotel. As she moved, Abhi stared at me, and without saying anything, started walking.

"Hey I am sorry, but how could we have agreed to that? We don't know her. What if she kills us" I tried justifying myself.

Abhi shouted at me and said, "Just keep quiet! Only because of you I had to miss that opportunity. You should also have stayed with Prabhat at the hostel."

"Look, it was me because of whom we got to speak to her" I said. We smiled, laughed a lot and started walking towards a rock which was stood tall, acting like a divider between foreigner's beach and Indian beach. As we climbed on to the top of the rock, our topic of discussion was Carron.

"Hey was that girl's intention right to call us to her room?" Abhi didn't reply to my question and said, "Don't remind me of that. Just because of you, we missed the bus, Infact deluxe bus. We could have had so many new experiences today." I was about to kick Abhi for that statement when suddenly my cell phone, which was in my shirt's pocket, fell down on the rock and rolled over before it went inside the sea. I literally jumped from a good height to find my cell phone, but all my efforts went in vain. I asked Abhi to call my number to see if it rang so that I could trace it. But it was foolish of me to think so, as once it went inside the water, that too inside the sea, it was gone forever.

We both put in our best efforts but were not able to trace it. It was almost dark by then and when Abhi checked the time, we were late by an hour.

"Let's go yaar," said Abhi.

"It was a gift from my brother," I sighed.

It was my first cell phone and I lost it in the initial days of college. I was tensed. I didn't know what I would say to my brother or what should I say to my friends back at the hostel.

I was murmuring to myself when Abhi, out of the blue said, "Don't worry about friends back at hostel. You are going to become a hero."

"Hero? But how?" I asked.

He said, "You leave it to me, just manage what to say at your home and let's go back to the hostel now."

I also didn't find any more reason to stay there, so we started for our hostel and was very upset when I made a call to my brother from Abhi's number and gave him some other reason. I wondered what to say to him and how foolish would it sound to say that that we were at the top of a rock, talking about the girl who had called us to her room and while kicking Abhishek, it fell into the sea? But as always, my brother's support made me happy.

"Don't worry bro, you will get a new one soon," he assured me.

We were about to reach the hostel. It was already 8:30 pm by that time but our luck favored us as some guys were taking a walk after their dinner. We followed them and sneaked into our hostel, hiding from the warden. But by that time, dinner time was over and no food was left, so we had to sleep with an empty stomach. As we reached, our group mates caught us and started asking about our evening.

"Hey, did you guys go to the beach? And Soumitro, why have you switched your cell off?" asked Jassi. I was about to reply when Abhi interrupted me saying, "Guys, all of you, come to our room; something serious happened."

I was wondering what he was going to narrate and how was he going to do that. Only one sentence of his made me quiet and that was – "You will become a hero." Within five minutes, all my group mates assembled in our room and few other guys also joined them.

"What happened?" asked Jassi with enthusiasm. Once again, the moment I was about to reply, Abhi took the stage and spoke.

"You guys will be happy to know what our dear Soumitro has done."

Happy with what I have done? I was thinking while swiftly that thinking turned to vacuum, when Raj interrupted and asked, "Tell us quickly what he has done."

Abhi continued, "We went to Mahaballipuram, headed straight away to the temple and then we went to the Indian beach. As the place was over crowded, we went to sit on the top of a rock. A group of girls were playing in water and suddenly, one of them while playing went inside the water. We were watching all this from the top of the rock and all of a sudden, that girl shouted for help."

He continued, "You know, I was thinking what to do when suddenly I saw Soumitro jumping from that height and dive into the sea, putting his own life to a big risk; he pulled her out of the water. All her friends were standing at the shore, shouting for help, but no one had the courage to help that poor girl. But see, our Soumitro did it." Everyone smiled and clapped for this achievement of mine and I nodded my head as if it had exactly happened. After all, who doesn't want to be a hero?

But I was wondering why Abhi made me the hero. Everyone asked me so many questions, "Hey did you ask her name, college, phone number?" And again I was about to say something, but Abhi took the lead and said, "Hey you guys don't know the real thing."

I thought that the idiot was going to make me zero then. So I interrupted and said, "Abhi leave it now man. It was just my duty, being a human being; I should help people in need."

But Abhi cut me again and said, "You know, when he brought the girl on the sea shore, she was lying unconscious and a lot of water had gone inside her. So Soumitro pumped her stomach to bring out some water, but still when that thing didn't work, one of her friends asked him to blow air in that girl's mouth....and you know guys, Soumitro had to do that. Imagine! A lip lock!

"What?" Everyone looked at me and came forward to punch me.

And then followed so many words, "You idiot! You kissed a girl."

Few minutes later, I said, "Hey friends, I was just helping someone, that's it."

All my friends kicked my ass. A few of them kicked me twice or thrice, and went out of the room. But before leaving, everybody said, *"Soumitro, yaar tu to hero hai bey!"* (Soumitro, *you are a hero*)

I looked at Abhi, shut the door after everybody left and said…."What made you narrate this story that I kissed that girl? That too, lips to lip kiss! I will kill you Abhi!"

We both fought for sometime and then laughed out loud.

"You really made me a hero, Abhi."

We didn't have food that night, but that fun was enough to put food out of my mind. I recalled that Abhi had clicked some photographs as well. When I asked him to show the pictures, he said, "Forget it, I will show you tomorrow."

After repeatedly asking him to show the pictures, he handed over his cell phone to me. When I opened the photo folder, I was surprised. There were pictures of that girl alone and with Abhi. I was nowhere.

"Hey, where am I?" I asked.

"Try to see the single photos of that girl; you must be next to her, but not in the frame" he replied and laughed aloud.

I got so annoyed with stupid Abhi that I started chasing him from my room to every corner of the hostel. While running, he said, "It is your punishment for ignoring that offer and still if you make me run, I will tell all our friends what exactly happened at the beach."

I stopped, as I had lost my energy and who doesn't like to be a hero. He really had made me a hero in front of my group and that beautiful girl had got a place in my memory besides Abhi's cell phone.

The number 13

ભ

You may call it the first year's excitement, enthusiasm or the fear of getting ragged, that many of us didn't go outside the hostel premises to interact with others, not even with girls. What made me recall this day was the previous night's incident that happened in room number thirteen of the boys' hostel.

It was around 2 pm. We had finished lunch and witnessed an incident which made Sujit, a guy from Patna, a villain become hero for us. The food in our mess used to be horrible as every dish tasted sour. Be it rice, daal, vegetables or salad, one would find a lot of curd and curry leaves in it! *Dosa*, *idli*, *saambar* and *rasam* are at the top of the available menu, wherever you go across Southern India. In the hostel, we had a good number of students hailing from different regions. So it was Sujit who raised his voice and threatened the mess manager to serve North-Indian food, else the battalion was ready to go for a hunger strike. Hence it was the hot topic of discussion in our room, among Abhi, Prabhat and I who being among the top debaters were trying to judge what went right and what went wrong.

All of a sudden, someone knocked our door. Knock Knock .....

We were wondering who it was then, as it was time for all boys to sleep. With doubts in his head, Prabhat opened the door and found Chandu out there (our next door neighbor). He joined in our discussion and made himself comfortable on

Abhi's bed. Abhi was off to sleep by that time, in a half sleeved T-shirt and half pants.

Abruptly Abhi shouted at Chandu, "*Yeh kya kar raha hai be saley?*" (What are you doing, Idiot!)

His reaction drew our attention towards them and to our surprise or rather, I should say astonishment, we found Chandu moving his hands over Abhi's thighs. Despite repeatedly stopping him, he continued to do the same. I had read somewhere about guys similar to him, but that day I witnessed it as well. When Abhi's temper went out of control, he asked me to lock the door so that we could teach Chandu a lesson and he would not repeat it ever.

I have been mischievous since my childhood, so I promptly followed the instructions given by Abhi. Then, it was almost a gang rape with Chandu. We took off his clothes one by one (the way people strip). He could have protested against it strongly but the way he protested, made us continue with the same enthusiasm and we started painting his body with black shoe polish with the help of a brush. "It is too dark now, let us make it a bit fair," said Prabhat. Within seconds, black shoe polish was replaced by white. We were laughing out loud and carried on till we realized that it was too much. We let him go once he said sorry and assured us that he would not repeat anything like that in the future.

We went to the washroom laughing uncontrollably. As we entered the washroom, we saw that we were left with no other choice than fleeing from there. Chandu was standing naked in the washroom calling us close to him! We then realized that he was a guy well described as "*Mai aadmi hu aadmi se pyaar karta hu.*"(A man who loves a man) Thereafter, whenever we noticed Chandu, we either changed our path, or used to avoid dark places with him. It is always better to protect yourself from such guys if you are straight! And we are straight after all.

It was dinner time. Abhi, Prabhat and I were talking about the afternoon incident, as we were yet to come out of the "Chandu shock." None of us knew that the night's experience was about to be frightful, which we would never be able to understand, explain or justify.

There was a guy in our department, named Chetan (the one who always saw himself at the top, suppressing others). He had slipped from the stairs during lunch time the previous day. Sumit and I thought to ask about his health and went to his room. It was room number thirteen.

A guy of a height five feet and three inches, very thin in appearance but a hard working student was lying on his bed with oil smeared on his body to get relief from the pain. We decided to stay there for a while, one by one. Later on, some more friends also joined us in his room asking about his health and we began chatting amongst ourselves.

Though it was the month of October, it was thundering and it appeared to rain heavily the very next moment. So we thought to return to our respective rooms.

We were about to leave his room when suddenly the power went off. It was pitch dark like a new moon day. It was around 11pm, so we thought to wait till the power returned. Twelve of us including his roommate and with Chetan, we were thirteen people at that moment in his room. We had never thought or dreamt of the incident that was about to happen in that room, else we would have definitely fled from there. Chetan asked us not to leave the room before the power returned. Thinking that he might have been feeling scared, we obliged him.

Chetan was lying on the bed and we twelve friends were standing around the bed. Suddenly, what I heard made me think hard, "Did I hear it right??" Chetan's voice changed to a female's voice which said, "Don't go away from this room till the sun rises or else you all will be killed." This voice pierced everybody's ears over and over again. Each one of us looked at each others' face to confirm if that was what we all had heard. And from everybody's facial expressions, we got to know that it was heard by all.

I had heard about hypnotism but why did the twelve of us hear that female voice that night, I don't know. Were we all hypnotized? Many thoughts came to my mind at that time. Suddenly, that female voice had disappeared and Chetan was back to normal, with his own voice. But the next statement of his made all of us abnormal for rest of our lives...He said, "Few days ago, my sister met with an accident on a highway and it was she who entered my body. That is why you heard that female voice." He added to our shock by saying, that somehow we all had to make that spirit stay inside Chetan's body, else it would destroy everything and kill all of us, one by one. None of us wanted to be a part of this episode but unfortunately, we were into it by then. He then suggested us to bring some dry fruits without going out of that room. Few of us were very nervous and dead scared. We haphazardly started searching through his room to get some dry fruits. Chetan said that we all had to control that power or energy by putting our best efforts and not allow him (Chetan) to get up from the bed. That meant, till he was sleeping, we were safe, else we would be killed one by one. In order to control him, we were supposed to put those dry fruits into his mouth. He warned us, "Do whatever you can to stop that energy going out of this room, but don't hit my head."

I had never believed in devils or evil spirits but that incident that night, made me believe in them. With every passing minute, that belief grew stronger. When I looked at Chetan, he had slept by then. Just a minute ago, he was talking to us very normally. He suddenly shivered and we felt some energy enter his body, which was so strong that the twelve of us together, putting all our efforts were not able to control him. This happened once, twice, thrice and many times. He held the neck of someone among us trying to kill him while the rest of us put in all our hard work to save him from that evil soul.

Each one of us, who was in the room, was giving his hundred percent because everyone feared that the very next moment, he might be the victim who would need the hundred percent of others to be alive. It was Sumit who was standing next to me at that time. No one was aware whose turn would it be next, whose neck Chetan's hands would be holding subsequently? I was also terrified and was thinking of my Mom to get some power to face the situation. Some of us were murmuring *Hanuman Chalisa* while few others were chanting *Gayatri Mantra*. By that time everyone was frightened; be it a guy weighting eighty kg or somebody as tall as six feet. Sumit was murmuring *Hanumam Chalisa*, without knowing that it would be his turn next, when Chetan's hands approached him suddenly. Sumit's voice and tone changed and he was trembled like anything. He continued chanting Hanuman Chalisa, but in a prolonged sing-song tone "jaaaaiiii hannnumaaannn gyaaannn…"

It was midnight by then; we came to know about the time by the beep of Abhishek's watch, which used to make that noise in every one hour. At that very moment Chetan asked us to look outside the window. We all turned our faces towards the glass paned window, and to our shock we saw something which shook the Earth beneath our feet. We saw the shadow of a running girl trying to pass through the window to get outside. We also heard the sound of her bangles very clearly.

Electricity resumed by half past midnight. I was not able to handle the strange things around me and my head buzzed with pain. Thanks to Sumit, who fainted suddenly or else I could not have come out of all this, till the first ray of Sun appeared the next morning. We were worried and were not able to think any further what to do. Chetan (now known as baba by all of us) asked us to take Sumit to his room. He was unconscious, so Vikash and I carried Sumit to his room.

We helped Sumit to sleep in his bed and gave him water to sip. It took about an hour for him to regain consciousness. Sumit's roommate was not there at that moment, otherwise everything would have been revealed to the entire hostel. *Baba* had asked us not to share that incident with anyone till we leave the hostel.

He also said that, the place where the hostel was built used to be a graveyard several years ago. I have no clue, what made all of us believe him and stay in the room but we were there doing exactly what he made us to do. I asked Vikash to return to our room once Sumit slept. It was about 2:00 am by then. I had thought that in Room number thirteen, things would be getting repeated, but Vikash and I got lucky due to poor Sumit.

I was literally trembling when I retired to my bed. I was not able to get over the incident. Was it a part of some horror movie, or a bad dream? But my eyes were open and it was surely not a dream. But few questions haunted me yet again - How come a single guy, that too who was so tiny and thin, was controlling twelve guys who were much taller and healthier than him? No medicine would have given generated such energy and why was there a power cut when there used to be no power failure in our hostel? Who was that girl running in boy's hostel or were we all hypnotized or was it something related to the unlucky "Thirteen?" There were thirteen guys in room number thirteen! All these questions came to my mind over and over again, till I slept.

Next morning, none of us discussed this issue with anyone, not even among the twelve of us. Chetan was known as *Baba* thereafter and my questions remained unanswered – What was that last night incident? Next morning when Prabhat told me to change the date in the calendar, I was surprised to notice the date which was also 13th the last night.

That is how the revenge was taken!

℘

I don't know whether Jaspal or anyone else was aware of her message to me, but I was very much aware and was desperately waiting for the moment when I could revenge her.

We both had each other's contact numbers by then, but I knew that none of us would contact each other. Our egos were too big for that.

Days were flying and the boys' gang were enjoying each and every moment of hostel life.

Every day around 8:00 pm the warden used to come for a round to check whether or not we were studying. 7:00 to 8:30 pm were supposedly our study hours, but the occupants of room number five didn't believe in abiding by the rules. Of course, the text books were meant to be there in our hands, but the Warden never dared to check what hid beneath them; story books, magazines, comics, novels. Reading material of all kinds was exchanged among us.

By God's grace, we always succeeded in "Mission Novel" during the study hours, till that day when the warden entered our room, without a warning. Prabhat and I somehow escaped but Abhishek was so much engrossed in the Magazine "Debonair" that even his good stars couldn't save him from getting caught.

As expected, he called Abhi in the meeting room, and like good roomies, we too accompanied him for moral support.

Light! Pitch! Sound! Action! Warden's Rapid Fire of logical

as well as illogical questions and Abhishek's single answer to all, "Sorry Sir."

Since that was the first time, he was given a warning and the magazines were seized from him.

We all hoped that he would study hard after what happened that day, but on the contrary to what we thought, our daring Abhishek again gathered all his courage to steal the seized magazine from the Warden's room! But the day didn't seem to be in Abhishek's favor and the moment he was about to enter the Warden's room, to his surprise or shall I say, "to his shock," the Warden himself was standing by him.

He was good at making excuses, and he made a good excuse that he had came to apologize as he was feeling really ashamed of what happened the night he was caught. Though he escaped the severest of the severe punishments he could have been subjected to after his attempt to steal that Magazine, that day onwards, the warden started keeping an eye on him. Even Abhishek started keeping his ears and eyes open; who wants a scolding in front of close friends and not so close friends either!

That day I remember Abhishek was abusing the warden like anything and he determined that by hook or by crook, we would take revenge from the warden. So it was certain that during the power cut from 9:30- 9:45pm, we would cover the warden with a blanket and kick him- left right center. Our plan was in place and we decided to execute it with all means. It was a Friday and we had the next two days as off. We decided to take advantage of "TGIF" (thanks God it's Friday).

As usual we finished dinner and came to our room, waiting desperately for the power cut. The power went off and we were stood hiding right behind the door, awaiting the warden to pass the corridor. (Habitually he used to take a round at that time). We heard footsteps approaching and were ready to act. And then as per our plan, we threw a blanket over him and started kicking like anything. I prayed to God to help us in the action and hoped the power not to resume any soon; else we all would get caught red handed.

On the contrary to what I thought, the power returned. Damn! We couldn't run or move. We got trapped. Our plan failed.

He came out of the blanket.

"Oh noooooo…." shouted Prabhat.

It was Anil and not the warden. Our plan had failed but thank God it was Anil or else we might have been wedged and the consequences would have been much worse. We laughed and the incident created evergreen memoirs of our hostel life.

Days were passing by happily, and nights at the boys' hostel even more happily. Anil was recovering from those unintentional kicks he received from us. I still bear in mind the daily power cuts between 9:30 and 9:45 pm after that night of 13th October. We all, along with the warden, used to go for a small walk.

Our hostel was in an open area compared to the girls' hostel, which was surrounded by gigantic walls. That night, Raj found a dead snake in the field. He played a prank on me. He folded the snake in a circle and handed it over to me. I screamed at the top of my voice and passed it on to someone else. The silly dead snake made everyone scream out of fear. It was quite dark and it was great fun to see all boys screaming; as boys are supposedly not afraid of anything.

Everybody was back to their rooms, as soon as the power resumed. Something naughty came to my mind, and I managed to get a polythene bag, kept that snake in it and without bringing it to anybody's notice kept the same in my bag.

Next day, as usual, we all went to attend our classes. During lunch hour, each one of us used to go to the canteen, playground, store or even library to spend time.

I was fully prepared for the revenge from Aastha. By that time, I could recognize her seat and bag. Nothing could stop me then and as intended, I immediately entered her classroom with the plastic bag. On seeing the classroom absolutely empty, I courageously placed that plastic bag with the dead snake beneath her desk. My work was accomplished. Knowing the fact that nobody had seen me picking the snake and keeping it there, a smile flashed on my face and I was happy to think that I had made a good retort to whatever she did to me.

The clock ticked 1:45 pm, and the "post lunch class" was about to start. Everyone returned to the classroom. When I saw her coming towards the classroom, I rushed back to my class & seated myself innocently. I was imagining how her response would be... Runaway, Scream, Cry... but above all I was confident that this time she would certainly get a good reply.

"Aaaaaaaaaaaaaaa..." someone screamed. The noise came from section-A. People rushed to that room. I knew why and from where that yell originated, yet I joined the crowd so that no one could doubt me for whatever happened.

I never wanted that to happen! Her nose was bleeding; her hand was bleeding. She was bleeding profusely. How did that happen? It was a dead snake. How did she hurt herself? She had fainted. Her friends supported her. She was taken to the medical room!

Jaspal and Abhishek recalled seeing the snake last night but of course couldn't figure out how it entered the classroom! I had never meant to hurt her. I never wanted to revenge her in that manner. I was feeling guilty but couldn't confess, because the punishment could be "Suspension from College." When I inquired about the entire incident, I got to know that after entering the classroom and taking her seat, she was about to take out her notebook from her bag. The plastic placed there caught her eye and as soon as she opened it, she screamed and ran away from there out of fear. On the way, she tipped over to be wounded badly!

I was feeling ashamed. I rushed to the medical room and heard everyone cursing the "nonsense" guy who did that. No one knew that the same nonsense guy was present among them. I waited there for two hours till I found she got a bandage over her nose and right hand. Her room mates supported her to take her to the hostel. Perplexed I thought "Should I talk? Should I say sorry?" I couldn't muster enough courage to do so, hence followed them quietly and said, "Please take care."

The entire night I felt guilty of what I did. I had never meant to counter her in that manner. All my friends were discussing the horrible incident. How did that snake enter the classroom? Who took it there?

I don't know why, but I didn't have the nerve to confess that it was I who had placed it beneath her table.

The next day she didn't turn up for her classes. I asked her roommates about Aastha and found that she was suffering with high fever. I still wanted to say sorry but how? I didn't have an answer to that.

That day I called her for the first time. She was unwell, that was quite apparent from her voice. She spoke to me for a few minutes.

I don't know what it was, but there was something that wanted me to change everything. I started asking about her well-being by calling her and sending text messages to her, almost daily. She was not recovering quick, and I was getting worried. I had an electric heater on which I used prepare tomato soup. I took the soup along with medicines and went to her hostel to give it to her. Since she was unable to come downstairs, I called her roomies to come downstairs and collect the same from me.

That's how the revenge was taken, but I didn't want to take it this way.

An Expensive night with Ria.

୧୪

A fter that revenge, I felt guilty for whatever happened. So I initiated an idea one day with my group to go out of the hostel to watch a late night movie just for a change. I thought it would help me forget about the guilt which I had been feeling. Not everyone was convinced by my idea, yet there were few who wanted to go.

So it was Abhishek, Sumit, Anil and I who decided to escape from the hostel after dinner and attendance.

As per our plan, we chose to implement the idea on that Friday. It seems when you pre-plan something, the waiting periods looks much lengthier. That week, from Monday we impatiently counted the days passing by. Four days to go, three days to go, two days to go, one day to go and finally the much awaited Friday arrived. The whole day passed by in the college, and after returning from our classes at 4:00pm, we planned to sleep for two hours, so that we could enjoy the whole night.

As the clock struck 6:00pm, we rushed to the washroom to get ready. Sumit was in the process of packing some clothes and towel in his backpack. Anil said, "Hey guys, we are not going there for any party or stay. So make sure that none of us takes any bags or else we may get caught at the main gate."

Everyone nodded their heads to show their agreement and I followed the same. Hence, as per the last meeting which we had in our room, we were supposed to go out in different groups after dinner and attendance, and thereafter assemble once we were out of campus.

With a neat plan in our heads, Sumit and I took a different route while Abhishek and Anil took another. If we would have boarded a bus from outside our college campus, the security guard at the gate would surely have got suspicious. So we planned to walk across the field to some distance until we would reach the main road for the next bus stop from college which was hardly a kilometer. In that dark night, nothing was visible apart from few vehicles which were passing by the main road. As we had divided ourselves into groups, it was Sumit and I who reached the bus stop first, expecting that others would take hardly five to ten minutes to reach there.

"Why the hell, are these guys are getting so late?" said Sumit.

"God knows. If they are about to start then we should not call them else the ringtone will alert everyone around and they would get attention of all other people out there," I said.

So we tolerantly waited for few more minutes before calling. Five..ten..fifteen..twenty minutes had passed, yet they were nowhere in sight.

"Have they changed the plan or did they get caught while coming?" I asked.

"Hey, I am also standing where you are," Sumit replied irritably.

After a long wait of thirty minutes, we considered to call Prabhat or Jassi and at least find out if something wrong might have happened. The phone rang. It was Jassi.

"Hey buddy where have you guys reached?" He put his question before I could start.

When he came to know that we had not even started, he started laughing out loud. I felt all the more angry with him and disconnected the call. Nothing was working out it seemed. Finally, Sumit called up Anil and shouted at him.

"You Fu*K*r, where are you guys?" I could hear it well the way he replied.

"You beep beep beep (Censored words) where are you guys getting yourselves f*ck*d?"

After Anil and Sumit's debate, I took the phone and tried to find exactly where they were at that point in time. We were surprised to find that they guys were waiting at the bus stop, exactly the previous bus stop which was then two kilometers away from where we were positioned. That day I got to know the importance to let one another know the reference point from where you can decide which one is right or left, because always right is not right and left is not left. I guess it was almost 9:00 pm and as it was very dark which left nothing visible, so we decided rather than walking and then meeting those guys, we would wait for the bus so that if one team gets into it, the other could get into same bus at the next stop. It was Anil and Abhishek who got into the bus and called us first. After their call we were assured that we would be together to decide night outing plans buttttttttttttttttttttttttttttttttttttttt............

The bus did not stop at the bus stop where Sumit and I had been waiting. Anil called me immediately to ask why we didn't board the bus. I got furious and hurled abuses at him once again.. beep beep..beep. Such an illogical question in that situation had really put me off.

"How foolish is he! The bus was running at 60kilometers per hour, without pausing and he is asking me why we didn't get on the bus," I yelled at Sumit.

Sumit called Abhishek and said to him, "You both get down from the bus at the next stop."

"It seems we would do this till the morning and then go back," I spoke in a fit of anger to Sumit.

Sumit kept his cool and acted calm.

"Don't worry, there is one more bus and if we don't catch that, we would return to our hostel. So we won't have to give repeat the performances till the morning."

Then we had to think how we would reach the next stop where Anil and Abhishek were waiting for us.

"Let's ask for a lift in some vehicle for the next stop," Sumit suggested.

"That's a good idea!" I exclaimed. After so much of fight, we all assembled at the Alathur bus stoppage and eagerly looked forward for the last bus to come.

Once the four of us met, it was the beginning of fun once again. Post twenty minutes, the bus arrived, and we boarded the bus in the two by two seat. The Bus was almost packed after we got into it; Chennai was some fifty kilometers from there which meant it was an hour long journey. We thought of remained seated and take some rest to restore our energy for the fun at night which we had planned. Abhishek and I were together on a seat. We heard few some female voices in the bus somewhere from the first few seats. The chemistry amongst Sumit, Anil and I, flowed through eyes, indicating each other how to find about the girls. Obviously, nobody had a clue then, how to go about it. But, as always, Sumit was the best person to look forward to in such a situation. Unexpectedly, he raised his voice and said in Hindi, "Driver *bhaiya*, can you please switch off this light?"

There was nothing extraordinary in his statement, but it made those girls turn around in surprise, as it was rare to find Hindi speaking people in Tamil Nadu. That curiosity of the girls to look back made it clear to four of us that they could understand Hindi and by their looks we could make out they were North Indians. But where were the girls going and with whom were they? These questions were unanswered till then.

The bus speeded on the roads when suddenly the driver applied brakes and screeched to a halt. There was huge cloud of dust outside.

"Everyone please get down. One of the tyres has blasted," said the conductor.

It seemed to us that destiny wasn't our side that night and not willing to let us go for the outing. Luckily, this incident took place besides a *dhaba*, so we quickly got down and ordered four cups of tea. We noticed six beautiful girls getting out of the bus. We saw a seventh person who followed the girls who looked like a mother or a teacher or may be a warden but we were sure that this lady was with them. It had become quite clear to us that in order to talk to those girls, it was important to win the heart of that lady. However, how to do that was a big challenge.

So for the time being, we all had to concentrate on that lady. Each one of us tried to impress her by whatever means we could think of but it looked like that the plan was not working out. In the meanwhile, we overheard a discussion between the beautiful girls and the *Dhaba* owner. None of us wasted a single moment and without looking here and there went straight to the shopkeeper and got ourselves involved into it. That heated up discussion was turning out to be violent. What made each of us more aggressive was that the shop owner was trying to talk trash with the girls.

The lady had also joined in the debate, and someway the argument cooled down, cooling the temperature over there.

All four of us were able to strike a conversation with the lady by then. When she asked us where we guys were going, four different answers from us made her little suspicious, which was natural. But god knows what made her believe Sumit's story that our parents were supposed to come to the station and we are going to receive them. When we saw she was convinced by Sumit's lie, we said "yes" after each question she put to us. And to make Sumit's point much stronger we added that our parents would arrive in Dhanbad- Allepey Express, which used to reach at 4 am in the morning and it was almost midnight by that time.

Her next statement actually froze us for a while when she said they would board the same train as they were going to Allepey for a competition there. We were sure that by any means we had to be with this group till 4:30 in the morning if we wanted to prove ourselves right and interact further with the girls.

The lady of the group all the girls and introduced us to them. "This is Mrinalini, Sapna, Shanti, Cauvery, Roopa and that is Ria."

I don't know whether it was her name or her looks which attracted me towards Ria for a long time! While I was lost in my dream I found my friends shaking hands with the girls and introducing themselves. My dream made me lose that opportunity as the conductor announced that the bus was ready to go and asked us to get in.

So the girls, the lady and we guys got onto the bus for the rest of journey. We had shuffled the positions on our seats and the girls sat right opposite to where we were. There was more than half an hour's journey left. So while the bus was in full velocity, my eyes were continuously looking at Ria and probably Ria was also looking at me.

After fifteen minutes I found that the lady had slept. At that time I was seated besides Abhishek who was seemed interest in Mrinalini who was sitting next to Ria. So with mutual understanding I asked Abhishek to let me swap the seat with Mrinalini so that I could get to know about her.

Abhi literally kicked me and said, "Good style to let someone know you but I am not going to try."

I was also feeling odd how to ask a girl whom I had known only for fifteen minutes to swap the seat with me. What if she reacted abstractly and how do I start. I had to do something. Then I happened to turn around found Anil sleeping while Sumit had already started gossiping with two-three girls seating besides his seat. I think it was his action or my own motivation, that I opened my "write message" folder in my phone and wrote,

"Would you mind if I ask you to come to my seat. I feel like vomiting and my friend doesn't want to leave his window seat" and passed on the phone to Mrinalini.

I looked from the corner of my eyes and saw her smile after reading the message. Then she returned me my phone. By then the screen of phone had locked and when I unlocked the keypad, I was surprised to see what she wrote.

"That's a nice style but make sure you do vomit" and a smiley followed.

Anyhow, my trick worked and we exchanged our seats. I could not imagine that such a beautiful girl with a great body posture and silky black hair was sitting next to me. It seemed as if she was feeling sleepy. I wondered how to keep her awake.

I was thinking what to do next when I happened to looked at Abhishek. He and Mrinalini were comfortable with each other and were indulged in talking. With so many thoughts running in my mind, I could not start a conversation with Ria. Suddenly, the bus started crossing a rough bumpy road. The jerks in the bus were also visible in her body and that too was diverting my mind. I had heard people saying when you get diverted, to control such feelings, close your eyes for a while and take a long breathe. I did the same and when I opened my eyes I saw her eyes were open too and she was staring at me. Our eyes met and we laughed.

This is how we started talking to each other and in the next half an hour we began to know each other.

We asked questions like what we were doing and our likes and dislikes and so on. And I don't know how, but in just a span of fifteen minutes, it was appeared as if we were very close friends as she was pushed me whenever I pulled her leg. One thought came to me about the kind of a person she was. But I didn't put my grey matter into this analysis and started getting close to her.

Whenever she said anything funny, I too pushed her and even touched her thigh at times. I thought she would react but her expression was normal, as if she was ok with it. In fact, she was quiet comfortable. So the next fifteen minutes were unlike anything I had ever imagined. She kept her head on my shoulder and said, "Can I rest my head for few minutes."

She also held my hand. If I had said no, I would have been the most foolish boy in this world. The way she was sitting so close to me, had anyone seen us, they would have considered that she was either my wife or girl friend. I didn't know if there was something wrong but I was ignoring this thought every time. The bus continued speeding on the roads when suddenly we crossed a tunnel and she held me tight. Before I could say anything, the short journey through the tunnel was over and by that time she withdrew her hands which were holding me tight in that dark tunnel.

Should I say thanks to the tunnel or wait for the next one, I could not decide.

Her hand was over my thighs and my hand was over her hand as I was not aware where would she stop. It was getting hard for me to control myself, but thankfully, the bus reached Chennai central station and we had to get down.

I thought our journey would end here, but there was something else written by the stars.

When all of us had de-boarded the bus, Ria said to the lady, "Mam I need to withdraw some money. Can I take Soumitro along with me?"

I was surprised to hear this from her and all my friends were wondering how come in an hour's journey I had won her trust. Her madam was cool so she didn't disagree. I was with her walking on the gloomy street and thought what if that was Delhi or any other place, would have I been able to walk this safe at 2:30 am with a girl? Suddenly she held my hand and said – "Hey we need to cross the road. That ATM is on the other side."

When I asked her to go inside the ATM room while I waited outside, she gently slapped my cheek and pulled me inside the ATM room, and gave me her bag to hold for some time. I was standing beside her and looking at her, wondering why she was doing all this. She was wearing a short red top and blue jeans. Before withdrawing the money, her ATM card fell down and before I could bend and pick it up, she bent to reach for it. The red T-shirt she was wearing was so short that while she bent down, I could see her milky white skin.

She said to me, "Do one thing, give me this stuff and withdraw the money." I was surprised that she was ready to give me her ATM pin code.

When I entered her pin 1432, I asked how much money she would need. She said, "Two thousand rupees. I don't want to burden my parents as we middle class family."

When I entered the amount on the ATM screen, and pressed enter, the screen's pop up showed "Insufficient amount."

I was a little surprised. I checked the amount in her account. She was left with just two hundred rupees. As the amount displayed on the screen, I looked at her face which had turned very dull, as if she would cry the very next moment. When I asked her what happened, she narrated me her story that her father was about to deposit two thousand rupees but quite possibly due to his less earning or some problem, he could not do that. Ria had started crying by then.

I was not comfortable with the tears of a girl. I offered her help, saying ,"Hey, don't worry I will give you the money. Just don't worry."

She ignored once, twice, thrice but when I kept saying, "Hey we have become good friends so there is no need for you to worry and you can return the money to me whenever you feel to do so."

I withdrew the amount from my account which had enough cash (but that was savings from my pocket money) and gave it to her. As I gave her the money, tears rolled down her cheeks and she hugged me inside the ATM room.

The temperature of the air conditioned ATM room was low and the room was chilled. But getting a hug from a hot and beautiful girl, at 2:00 am in the morning was enough to make my body temperature go high. I felt warm.

For almost two to three minutes, she hugged me and looked into my eyes. I thought about taking a step ahead. I brought my face close to her. A little closer again, and my lips were an inch away from hers. I closed my eyes. She kept her eyes open as she was aware of what she was doing, but I was not aware of what I was going to do next. I felt her breath and as her lips were about to touch mine, something beeped.

"Tringggggggg, tringgggggggg……"

It was her cell phone and we got detached that moment.

Bullshit! What a time to call and who was the caller? That lady!

"We are coming in two 2 minutes," she answered and disconnected the call. Holding my hand, she said "Hey, let's go fast."

I followed her and in soon in five minutes we reached the waiting room. I saw Sumit was still busy talking to girls and Abhishek was in a dark corner with Mrinalini. We spent the next one hour talking to each other but Anil was not there. "Where is Anil?"I asked others.

"He has gone for a peg," replied Sumit.

Everyone wanted to spend time the way they felt comfortable. It was 4:00 am and the train was on time. We all went to platform number five, fifteen min early, to see-off the girls and as per a lie to accompany our parents. The lady said, "Hey, you guys can leave and can take care of your parents. We will now easily board the train." But the three of us, didn't want to miss the last glimpse of those girls.

We convinced her that we would get a call once our parents got down from the train. Finally their train arrived and they boarded it. Trust me, I was thinking whether she had cheated me, or she was truly in a financial problem. But I could do nothing at that moment as I had already given her the amount. If I told my friends about it, they would have kicked me and said "We haven't seen a fool like you."

The girls boarded the train with the lady and made themselves comfortable in their respective seats. Ria took the seat next to the window while I stood outside watching her. She stretched her hands through the window and put them over mine. Finally the green flag waved off and train was about to start its journey. My journey with Ria would end soon, and so would for Mrinalini with Abhishek and Sumit with his girls.

The wheels of the train got in motion, started revolving slowly and I started walking beside the train on the platform. Suddenly I found a paper above my hand which Ria was trying to pass on to me. The train picked up its speed and I had no option but to leave the window and hold the piece of paper at least. I took the crumbled paper from her and put it inside my pocket.

All of us were sad for a moment but then within no time everyone was laughing. We then started looking for Anil and found him lying on a chair on the station platform. After getting to wake him up we planned to go to Marina beach to enjoy the dawn before we get back to the hostel. Marina beach was hardly a fifteen minutes drive from there. We got ourselves into an auto to reach Marina Beach.

The time was 5:00 am. Sky was yet not clea. We could hear the birds chirping. While walking on the cool sand near the beach, everyone discussed their experience with the girls and what all happened in details. At the end of every statement, Anil added his "Beep beep beep you crazy boys" and we three replied "You lazy boy." I told everything to my friends except what happened inside ATM as I thought to check the paper before disclosing the fact to them.

As I unfolded the little paper, there I saw a note written,

"Thanks for the financial help and moments spent with me. Hope we meet again" followed by a number 979104565.

I was happy to receive that number and immediately dialed it but the response literally broke my heart as it was said "Please check the number you are trying to call." When I checked, it was nine digits number. I didn't know how to react and whom to blame, whether it was intentional or a mistake. I didn't dare to narrate the real story to my friends or else they would have laughed at me. While coming back to hostel I concluded that the night was an expensive one with Ria.

CREA-That Cultural Evening

℃

The real fun or the excitement of engineering life would have not been completed without fests or the cultural nights. This was the second year when we had an unforgettable evening and the cultural event-CREA which have given so much fun and evergreen memories for many of us.

By that time our department had become quite popular, and known due to what we had done in the history of our University. There was a lecturer of the Electrical branch in our department, who had given us a tough time. For reasons unknown, the lecturer did not like us and we detested her as well. Every other day she used to have a debate or a never ending argument with anyone picked randomly among our batch mates.

Our understanding, rather our misunderstanding, went to such extremes, that she found it appropriate to vent it out on us during practical exams, as she was the one who handled our practicals.

About Eighty percent of our department students were given marks which were much lesser than the passing marks and I was one among them. Protests, letters and objection were made by us for almost ten days. It is truly said that one can only understand and make others aware if you are one of the victims of it and that stood correct for me.

Since I was also the victim, our words, our request and all the support from our batch mates made the management take the decision in our favor and a minimum slab was created. Above all, the examination papers were re-evaluated and thereafter many were awarded with much better, well deserved marks. Call it our luck, the lecturer resigned from her job .This is how we came into lime light in college and hence made our department well known by all.

We were then in the second year, hence we had to contribute much and our involvement was supposed to be more, compared to last year's event. Several houses were divided and each student was allocated a house. I was one among the vice-captains of the house. Gradually there were responsibilities on my shoulder since I had to handle all the students of first year. I got separated from my friends as they were allocated different teams. We thought to come up with a special performance all together since we felt creativity was in our blood. We always felt that anyway!

Sriram, Tuhin, Shailesh were quite artistic people who came up with an idea. "Why can't we do a theme based drama," said one among them. On which we all agreed and got a script which was based on SAVE EARTH, SAVE HUMANITY. I got the part of Changu- a police inspector to play with Sumit as Mangu, along with few South-Indian speaking students. We also had two people in our play, which had no dialogues. Subba, who had to play a statue, and Rejani handled anchoring. Preparations were at its peak. My priority was to boost up my house to give our best, as well as to give best efforts for the special performance by our department.

That was the time when Aastha and I had become friends. She had been assigned a different house but I could not figure it out why she had not participated in any event, be it sports or even cultural. On asking her the reason, she excused herself with the same answer that she did not like to participate, as she wasn't interested.

I could have believed her but every day when my house preparations or even our special event preparation was going on, she used to be with me, instructing, guiding and even enjoying. I could sense the happiness on her face and kept wondering whether really she didn't have interest in such activities or she had said so to be with me. I wanted to know, but couldn't.

We left no stone unturned for our preparations, when out of the blue, we came to know that our department's special performance was not able to find a slot. So it turned out to be impossible to showcase our performance. It was enough to demoralize us, since almost everything, costumes, script, roles, was ready at our end by then. We united again. It was Sriram and few of us who went to the program coordinator and requested her to allow our performance on stage.

With a lot of hassles, finally that program coordinator finalized that we had to finish our act in a maximum time of fifteen minutes, not even a minute extra. Reluctantly we had to cut short wherever we could.

The day arrived at last. Excitement and happiness persisted, since it was the day without a dress code, lot of surprises a fun-day out for us. Morning session was assigned for prizes and preliminary rounds for many other events. The real package was yet to come which was allocated for the evening slot, post sunset. I was tensed and worried for my house performance but found Aastha beside me at every step encouraging and morally supporting me.

During lunch break, Aastha complained of headache and wanted to return to the hostel. I walked with her till the hostel gate and asked her to take care of herself. On asking whether or not if she would come for the evening mega event, she replied with a "Not sure" gesture, and said she would join only if she felt ok.

I escorted her to the gate and returned to the premises. I was feeling bad about her sudden headache. I was not aware that her pain would leave me shocked in the evening. I went back to boost up my team members for their ongoing performance. Due to shortage of time, only the winners and runner ups of fashion show were given a chance to perform during night events.

Our houses were not fortunate to qualify, since Sriram house and Sanjay House were much talented and better to grab those places.

Gradually, the sun started disappearing setting the mood of the show with time. The day was about to end and so was my hope that she would come to see our performance when I received a message from her, "Sorry, wouldn't be able to turn up, I am not feeling well. All the best, I am going to sleep."

I immediately called her on her number, but she didn't attend my call. Once, twice, thrice she didn't answer my phone even once.

All that growing attachment suddenly abridged as I couldn't discover how a person could sleep so early. Was she ok? Or she did this deliberately to ignore me? If that was so, then why the hell for the last ten days she was with me, with my house to support me? Those questions buzzed in my head time and again.

Suddenly intervening my thoughts, Vinay said, "Dada get ready, we have less time now."

Vinit my roomie, my best pal, had recovered from Chicken Pox but he was with us in the performance and a mere headache

of Aastha, stopped her to be present that evening. I was angry
within, so much that I thought I would not talk to her anymore.
Time was running fast, my costume of police inspector was
in front of me. I was ready when Sumit (my Mangu-partner)
shouted, "Dada we need to paint or do something over Subba
(statue) to give him the original look."

I had no clue that it was Plaster of Paris which both of us
was going to put over Subba from top to bottom. I was not
even aware of the consequences. When I asked "Can we put
this on Subba?" to which he innocently replied "Go ahead"
with a hope that it would not affect his skin. I was confident
nothing would happen and with two kilos of POP in liquid
state, I painted him from head to toe. We all were nearly ready
with our respective costumes then. We were right behind the
stage waiting for our turn; unexpectedly we found that the
POP smeared on Subba had started to dry up and the pieces
falling off. Thankfully it was a perfect alibi since during the
play the statue had to be broken by all community people and
had to give the shape of their own God.

Then followed our turn; the Department of ECE to present
a special play.

"Let's welcome them," the announcement echoed on the
loud speaker. Hooting, thunderous sound of applause and
whistles followed. Most of our supporters were in the front
row among the audience. We had to be careful about the script
which was cut short and the actors were instructed the same.
But I didn't know what happened to Vinit, was it his illness or
his pro-activeness, he was so much indulged into the play that
he forgot the instructions. We kept indicating him from the
rear side of the stage to stop , but continued to speak, forgetting
his script.

Hinduism is what he had to speak about. He spoke non-stop till he was pulled back by Santosh. It turned out to be funny. The audience clapped and laughed out loud. Frankly speaking, it was beyond the script and had a serious message to convey. Somehow we had managed to give our message on time- Save humanity, Save Earth.

Vinit became the center of attraction for our group and his role became a joke for all. We realized suddenly that it was time to clean Subba as he was painted by POP and might have set in by this time. Simant and I took Subba to the washroom to help him remove the POP. It was then, that we came to know of the blunder we did. Despite drenching him in water, the POP had stuck to his hair. I could not think of any remedy then. Unfortunately he was left with a single option and that was to cut his hair. Subba had to leave for a haircut. We felt bad that for our play he had to leave the event in the mid way and had to sacrifice his hair. Later he was considered not less than a brave soldier in our department who had sacrificed his hair for our special event.

But the real story began later. I also changed my get up, went to the audience row to watch the rest of the program which had lot of fun and excitement left.

I saw my phone blinking with a message, "Can you come in front of Electronics lab now?" It was natural for me to be surprised, as the Electronics lab which was on the second floor was empty. All the students and faculty were at the stage premises. Then why and how was Aastha there calling me? I called her back but she didn't answer my call. She was ill sometime earlier, why did she go to the Electronics lab?

I was curious and confused. I headed for the Electronic Lab section. It was all dark there, I could not see anything. I called her number again, standing in front of Lab which was locked from outside. Surprise time it was for me as I noticed a mobile blinking outside the window of the lab. I went to see whose mobile it was. I saw the name "Bawarchi" on the screen. "Who the hell is this Bawarchi? And whose cell is this?" It didn't take long for me to know that my number was stored in the cell as "Bawarchi." But where was she?

I was gripped with anxiety what had happened to her, how did she reach there and how come her mobile was lying in middle of nowhere?

I couldn't stop thinking about her well being. Some wrong thoughts crept into my mind. I made up my mind to call her roommates to ask about her since I searched nearby but found nobody in the dark.

As I pressed a button in her cell, I saw the "Write message" folder where "come to 1st floor opposite library" flashed. I couldn't figure out anything that time, with various thoughts vibrating in my head. What was happening and why I was doing exactly what she asked me to do? While coming downstairs I thought of scolding her and "Bawarchi"- What made her give me this stupid name? I saw a guard coming upstairs, giving me a suspicious look.

I started running, but slowed down on seeing a group of boys near Library. I was waiting for them to vacate the place, so I hid beside the wall. Why were these guys there at that moment, I could not figure it out. Did they see the message in that cell or something else, I suspected.

My sixth sense gave me all reasons to worry. I was behind the wall for fifteen minutes till I saw those boys going downstairs. I took a breath of relief and rushed again near the library door, which was closed. I could not see anybody there but it was not dark. However, she was not there. I was fuming with anger with every passing minute and held my phone tight in one hand while hers in another.

I looked for her in the corridor, and every possible corner, but found nobody. My footsteps echoed. As I moved few steps ahead, I spotted something below my shoes. It was a piece of paper, where there was a note for me "Come inside girl's washroom door no. 2."

I couldn't figure out what was happening. Was she mad or what or was it someone else? I asked myself, "Should I go into the washroom?"

"No, never!" buzzed my mind. So I thought to call her roomies once to know what the matter all about was. I called them one after another but none of them answered my call. I tried a number of times but didn't get response from anyone. I thought it was better to go downstairs instead of entering a ladies washroom. What if someone catches me, what if I find any other girl inside the washroom..I almost panicked. But probably it was girl's attraction or something else that I started walking without knowing the consequences or even without knowing what I was doing. I closed my eyes and marched towards washroom which was at the end of the floor in a corner.

I moved two steps further when abruptly I heard a known voice laughing loudly. I turned back. What I saw was never seen before. Should I shout, should I beat, should I hug? It was Aastha, standing beside a wall and laughing out loud. I ran towards her to shout at her and ask why did she do so, but couldn't speak.

I was pleasantly surprised and my expression of happiness was out of this world. She was clad in a saree. It glittered and she appeared like an angel from the heaven. I had never seen her in this kind of getup. My eyes were wide open and constantly watched her even without blinking.

She was laughing loud but I couldn't hear her. I stood there, stunned.

I hadn't seen her ever like that ever before. I was lost in some other world, but got back as she took her cell from my hand and asked, "How was the surprise?"

I could not say anything... I was speechless for a while. All I wanted to say was "Nothing can be as beautiful as you look now."

I then said to her, "Let's go down to see the last performances at least." While we were walked down the stairs, I asked her, "What made you store my name as Bawarchi'? She laughed again but did not reply. I made a guess that possibly it might be the tomato soup which I made for her when she was ill.

She appreciated our act on the stage, which she had watched with her friends sitting right in the front row of the audience. Yes, it was all pre-planned. We enjoyed that evening and those memories remained alive forever.

That Dark Night....

࿔

"Life is a mirror, reflecting what you do, if you care for someone, they will care for you" this statement proved absolutely correct for me after that cultural night. The name "Bawarchi" was turning appropriate for me as whenever I got chance to cook for her... My wife would be the happiest to have the world's greatest cook as her husband- I often used to say this to my friends..!

She was much more intelligent than me and a damn hard working girl, but what had made her call me that evening was still not known to me. Once she said that she had doubts in Electronics Devices and wanted my help! Taking help from somebody who himself didn't know the "E" of Electronics Device!

Second years exams were knocking the door, or should I say hitting the door!!!

So this new lecturer, of course me, went through the problem thoroughly and took many of my friend's help and explained it to her over the phone. Cell phone turned out to be a pillar of strength or you may call the backbone of our relation, since from that day till the last day of our tenure in college, we became habitual of studying together over the phone. Initially it was two or three hours a day, but later it became twenty four by seven by three hundred and sixty five days business!!!

We chose Reliance as our telecom partner, as it valued relationships as well as it had the minimum traffic plan among all the other service providers. One always had to check one's pocket and when it is about students it stands very true!

Chennai, a place where temperature and humidity are always high, receives the retreating monsoons which are sometimes very destructive. On the 26th day of December 2004, Tsunami destroyed many lives and families. The horrible incident was fresh in the memories of those who were present there at that time. I considered myself to be lucky enough to have witnessed it through newspapers and television rather than being a victim.

But I was not aware that next year I would be in that same city with something like that to happen again.

I still remember it was raining continuously for the last four- five days. The whole place was water logged, be it our playground, or nearby areas. I was on my bed in room number five watching the horrid rains through the window which was next to my bed.

Our college had declared holidays from the last three days due to heavy rain. Abhishek came to me and exclaimed "*Yaar college ne lambi holiday declare kar di*" (The college has declared a long holiday)

We all ran towards warden's room to see the notice board. It was no less than a fish market when we saw the notice, which read, "It is hereby declared that college will remain closed till further notice. The hostel residents are requested to vacate the premises in the next 24 hours, as instructed by the Government" We started discussing among ourselves -What do we do now, how do we vacate the hostel so soon and from where would we get the tickets and so on. Without much of thinking we had to pack and leave soon.

So we decided to start by 3pm that day itself since there

used to be a mail train for Howrah at 11:30 pm from Chennai central.

"But how will we start in the rain?" asked Jaspal.

"We will manage, let's pack our stuff." I said and came to my room.

Once I entered the room my phone started ringing. Those were calls from girls who had also got the same notice and had to leave for the same destination where we were going. So they wanted to go along with us! I counted… 9,10 11,…14 (Eight guys and six girls), that meant a full cricket team with three reserved players…Then later it was their parents' turn to give continuous calls on my cell… "*Beta dhyan se aana*" (please be careful while coming) and so many other words which made me feel how important I was for them, at least during the tough time!

More important than anything else, they wanted me to take care of their daughters…I never felt as if it was a burden since I am capable of managing all such situations easily and Jaspal also supported me well, whereas rest of my friends kicked my ass whenever they could!

Anyhow, our team of fourteen moved out of our hostels sharp at 3pm. It was still raining. We sheltered ourselves under umbrellas and walked towards the main road. Bus number 119 to Koyembedu Bus stop, was only the direct route from the hostel to the railway station. We all got seats in the bus, as there were very few passengers who were forced to go out in this heavy rain. Every now and then I could feel the tyres of the bus running through puddles of water on the road. We were absolutely unsure of what was about to happen next, and feared whether or not we would be able to board the train.

It thundered loudly, hence making the situation more challenging for us. The bus stopped suddenly. After an effort of twenty minutes, the driver asked us to get down. Water had seeped into the engine. We all got down with our heavy bags. The girls were carrying two bags each! *Women!*

As I got out of the bus, Aastha looked at me for help. How could I have denied that request which she made with her eyes? So I carried her bag and somehow managed to get under a shed. All of us were almost drenched except Raj who was carrying a rain suit. There was no bus in sight. We hired a big sized auto rickshaw, which was basically used as carrier van. We didn't even bother to ask the fare amount to be paid and boarded the auto rickshaw. Jaspal and I took the two extreme ends of auto, where half of our bodies were outside the auto. Partially we both got sopping wet and the rest of my buddies enjoyed the compact journey!!

We arrived at railway station by 8:30 pm. We felt content that the struggle would be over once we get into the train. But we all realized that we did not have tickets with us, so Abhishek and I rushed to get tickets from current reservation counter while Jassi and rest helped the girls to manage their language at one corner of the entrance. The announcement made by railways was a shocking one for us.

"All trains leaving Chennai central have been cancelled for two days. Sorry for the inconvenience caused"

They felt sorry and we felt helpless. When asked, we came to know that due to heavy rain, the bridge collapsed which was on the route for all Howrah bound trains. We scratched our heads, and after exchanging a lot of dialogues, we settled to stay in a hotel for the night to see what best could be done next. So it was Jaspal and Prabhat who went to search for hotels. They took more than an hour before they came back to the station. Phone lines had got jammed and lost connectivity. 'No hotel, lodge or *dharamshala* are available in spite of paying double the amount.' They both were totally soaked in rain as they had to cross the water logged roads to reach the hotels. The three girls in our group decided to stay at their relatives place in Chennai. To our relief, they left.

The remaining eleven of us decided to spend that night at the platform after looking at the waiting room's condition where there was no space to put your foot down! That day I also realized the importance of birth control in India, wishing there were less number of people in those hotels so that we would have had one room at least, and could have sheltered ourselves from the rain and wind.

It was platform number two, where there was a less frequency of the trains. So we thought to occupy a corner on the platform. Anil suggested getting into the train which had been waiting for more than two hours there. It looked like that the train would also stay there for the whole night. "Let's go and get in," I said. But none of the girls showed their consent over that, as nobody knew the train could start any time. Hence with a common consent, we premeditated to spend the whole night at the platform. It was a big challenge for us to find whose bed sheets were still dry, since everybody's bed spreads were soaked in the rain. With no dry blankets or bed sheets, we spent the night walking and talking. The subsequent morning, we all smelled like fish due to wet clothes. It was not raining anymore then but the next question was "What to do next? Shall we go to Mumbai and then to Kolkata?" We all were looking for alternatives when that sudden announcement gave us a ray of hope.

"A special train has been arranged for all passengers going to Howrah."

We jumped with joy, as if that train was coming for us! We went to platform number nine where the train was about to arrive but again our happiness vanished into thin air when we saw three times the number of passengers of the train's capacity waiting at the platform. Since all colleges had vacated their hostels, the crowd was unimaginable. I went to buy general tickets for all, considering that the arrangement would be made once we get into the train. We call it *Jugaad*. I managed to get the tickets after being in the queue for more than an hour.

It was 9:30 am then.

I saw the rear side of the train entering the station. We had planned that four of us would go first to occupy the seats and then the rest would follow. The train came to a halt. I didn't even move my legs but I was inside the compartment. A huge crowd had pushed me inside the packed train where it seemed oxygen supply had been cut down. Survival had become tough inside! Four of us de-boarded the train and considered not to take that train, as it was next to impossible to travel in the jam packed suffocating box. It was a smart move by Abhinav who said, "Let's move ahead and get into any coach." Luckily we found eight seats vacant at the same place. We occupied the seats as if we had booked them for ourselves. Eleven people on eight seats, was not a tough task as Jassi, Prabhat, Anil and I adjusted in two seats. We arranged everything and thought that the journey would be comfortable without knowing that the real trouble was yet to come.

Most of our phones were switched off due to low battery and those which were still on, received frequent calls from parents. In the next two hours all our phone batteries gave away. Aastha was there with us among three other girls. I had a word with her parents and asked them not to worry. We waited for the TC who arrived around six in the evening. We gave him our general tickets and asked him to allot confirmed tickets. He said, "You will be penalized since you don't have sleeper class tickets."

We asked him the amount.

He replied "Eight hundred rupees."

We thought that eleven people paying eight hundred rupees, was fair enough. But the moment he said eight hundred rupees per head, we were taken aback, as paying a penalty of eighty eight hundred was quite a big deal and a matter of worry for us. Damn our *jugaad* turned futile!

None of us had so much of amount in their pockets. We requested him to adjust the amount, and finally we could convince him for four thousand rupees. It was his day after all! We were least aware of the train route, since that was not a normal route we used to follow. Nobody knew where we were. We spent the night singing and sharing jokes. The next day passed by in a similar manner, though we could not find out our exact location. Supplying drinking water and food was beyond the scope of pantry car. It was more than forty eight hours and we hadn't even reached half way! Normally, it would have taken twenty nine hours to reach from Chennai to Howrah.

The train halted at stations where we battled to grab *idlis*, from the hawkers, which were as hard as a stone, without *sambhar* or *chutney*. Before the train could enter any station, people rushed to the hawkers for food items. What is food deficiency and how tough is the life of people who have to sleep without food, was silently witnessed by all of us. We had been through an ordeal of fifty eight hours journey by then and we finally had crossed half the way. Vishakhapatnam it was. I called Aastha's mom from the station's PCO to inform her that her daughter was fine and requested her to convey the message to all other parents, as by that time all parents were in touch with each other to get information about their kids. Thanks to the inventor of telephones.

"It is fourteen hours more from here if it runs fine," said a pantry car boy.

Next day around 11:00 am we finally arrived at Howrah railway station, after a seventy two hours unforgettable journey. It was home for two of us in the group while the rest had to travel for five-six more hours before they got sleep on their beds at their homes. I was also one of them. I saw those relaxed and happy faces of Aastha's Mom and Dad who were at station by that time. They expressed their gratitude by thanking all of us to make their daughter reach safely.

I was exhausted, but had to get into my next train to complete rest of the journey. I got myself comfortable at a window seat and wished that such a night never come again.

Who was Babyjaan ?

༫

After the mess and ups and downs with the last journey, we were back to the hostel and studies picked up the momentum. Our telephonic studies and conversation had become a daily habit by then which continued smoothly. One day Prabhat objected to my conversation inside the room, since it was natural for my roommates to get disturbed. "How do I manage this now? It's so difficult to get rid of this habit now." I asked myself, and I got the same reply each time, "How would you survive Soumitro?" I was addicted talking to her over the phone. Seeing no alternative with me, I started studying with her, no not physically; through the same medium of cell phone, but the place was different.

Sometimes it used to be in the mess or stair case or even sitting outside somebody's room that was yet to switch off the light. When all lights were switched off somewhere around 12:30 am, we used to talk about everything apart from studies…!!

Our exams were approaching; we both studied all subjects, all pages together over the phone. I was confident while appearing for my exams since I had already done good preparation for every subject. At times I used to study with her outside my room with a candle while all boys used to go off to sleep by 2 am, but she never allowed me to sleep till we were over with revision, which sometimes continued till as late as 3:00 or 3:30 am! Results were declared and I scored well, from seventy two, my graph touched eighty percent. She was as usual among the toppers with eighty four percent in her score card. Intelligent girl, I must say! Studying together was turning out good for both of us.

After second year, we eight friends decided to leave the hostel. Why? Well, because we hated the mess food. Together we thought of vacating the hostel, but differences arose when Sumit and I denied staying away from college. Our college was away from the city, so rest of all decided to stay somewhere close to the city. Sumit and I made up our mind to stay at Paiyanoor, which was a kilometer away from college. The other people of my group went to Kelambakkam (fifteen kilometers away from college). Days did not remain the same anymore. There were no fights for getting entering the washroom first; no food was being served in the morning, afternoon or night. Sumit and I wanted to have food made at home.

Maids were not available there, so we had to cook on our own. Sumit was a lazy but crazy boy. He was a guy who hardly cared to take a shower in scorching forty degree Celsius temperature. He sometimes even ignored to change or wash his inners for three- four together! I found that disgusting! I used to wake up early, to prepare breakfast and fill the water tank, since there was no tap connection in the kitchen. It became my daily routine. Many a times I did express my anger (which was very much justified) and didn't even refrain from shouting at him; but Sumit did not change. However, I was enjoying my life that way, because I knew that I was close to her, just a kilometer away!!!!

Should I call it a rule set right for girls or not, but there were only two outings each month permitted for them, which later became my outings as well, as it was only me with whom she used to go for day outs. Be it the Sarvana Store at T Nagar,

Pondy Market or Marina beach; it was both of us spending time together. Can it be called love? Neither did I feel nor did she, and none of us confessed either! Whatever it was, we were enjoying each other's company. She was no more a rude arrogant girl for me. The girl whom I decided to avenge was no more that same girl. Aastha and I were defining friendship for ourselves, by that time.

One fine day she asked me, "Don't you love anyone? I mean, don't you have a girl friend?" I didn't know what should have been my reply. I was thinking to count the three incidents of the last two years when I defined love or should I say no?? I was perplexed and going through my thought process when she interrupted again, "O *Bawarchi*..tell me na…"

"Yes I do love someone. Her name is *Babyjaan*" I replied

Babyjaan – she laughed. I laughed too, since even I didn't know who *Babyjaan* was! She bombarded me with questions. How does she look, where does she reside, what was she doing then and blah blah….. Uff! I m telling you, these girls think a lot!

I responded to all her questions with imaginary answers. Days passed by smoothly and happily…

"You have to leave the room," said Sumit.

I thought he was joking, but he was serious!

"But why?" I asked him several times. He didn't reply. We had a quarrel that night.

I came to know the next day that Sumit wanted me to vacate the room due to that girl; a medical college student supposedly. I started searching for a new roommate then.

Vinit (a simple, spiritual, and down to earth guy who is one of my best buddies) became my new roommate. The day I shifted with him, I missed Jaspal and the gang. I could not go back to them because the distance between us had widened with time. Maybe I was the reason for it! Situation was different then and much different today. I convinced myself by saying so. That was the first time Aastha came to my room to help me in shifting. Since Sumit and I were busy in packing, she cooked food for us.

"Egg curry and rice are ready," she said.

That was the very first time she cooked something for me. Indeed she cooked so well that my mind buzzed with this thought - she would be the best Mrs. *Bawarchi*. In the evening at 4:00pm, Sumit went to call an auto in which I was supposed to transport my luggage; that black trunk, and so much stuff by that time! Finally I left Paiyanoor and started for Kelambakkam, now fifteen kilometers away from college and her.

Aastha's parents were very strict and possessive. I never asked her to shift to a Paying Guest (PG) House in Kelambakkam where many girls of our college stayed. I was in my new fully furnished flat with two bedrooms, a kitchen and separate toilets. This room was much better than previous one in every sense but only one thing which wasn't there, was those possibilities of evening walks and strolls after dinner together in college campus which we had got used to in the last one year!

I was delighted that my conversations with Aastha over the phone would not disturb Vinit. Should I call it his greatness or love for me that he never complained nor objected, though at times I felt that he was left alone, even when I was with him. We used to relax on the terrace, often chatting and exchanging views on various topics!

One of the topics which I never forgot was, "Is it the name or face which human beings forget first?"

I cannot forget, it was during the fifth semester periodic exams, she was suffering running high temperature. Chikungunya it was, I found later. She was not able to take a single step, but was strong willed to appear in the exam of "Microprocessor." I called it her insanity, and didn't allow her to sit for the exam. I even instructed her roomies to ask the warden to take her to Chettinad Hospital, which was close to my new residence. I knew college medical room was not enough to cure the disease. She repetitively told me that her Mom asked her to attend the exam and then go.

I have always valued humanity more than anything. I told her that I would get permission from her mother, and she need not worry. I don't know whether I took the right decision or not, but I did what I felt. Later on, when the doctor said if we had delayed a bit, she would have been admitted for a longer time. Her mother called me a number of times to ask about her health. I assured her of Aastha's well being and my company with her. Both of us didn't appear for the exam that day and frankly speaking, I was least bothered about it. I was with her, sitting beside her bed and holding her hand every time the doctor injected her, gave medicine or even saline water.

The lady warden gave me weird look. I wasn't concerned about her look either, since all I could feel was Aastha's pain and I was happy that I was trying to lessen it, by being close to her. She was the same girl for whom I had once said "*Mai to ghas bhi na dalu usko*"

The same girl who had replied to me in the message "*Apni behan ke liye*"

The same girl whom I wanted to take revenge from, but not in that manner…

She was the same girl in our gang of fourteen (Eight boys and six girls) for whom I had said,

"I can fall in love with any girl in this gang, but not with Aastha."

The memories of the past gripped me while I was sitting beside her when she was sleeping after a painful injection. All those hard feelings had washed away.

She was the same girl but my thinking had changed for her, she had taken a place in my heart then.

A very special place!

Gaining consciousness, she slowly opened her eyes asked me, "How is your *Babyjaan*??" I was shocked with her question. I had forgotten who was she. Within a fraction of seconds I recalled and replied, "She is not fine" and went out of the room to conceal my emotions from her.

The doctor called me to bring a dozen of medicines. I rushed to buy the prescribed medicines and brought some fruits with them. By evening, she was discharged from the hospital. The college ambulance had come to pick her. She was holding my hand. "Get into the van and drop her till the gate of girl's hostel," the lady Warden said. I was with her, clinging her hands tight and our eyes were talking to each other. I felt as if Aastha was asking me not to leave her hand ever in life. It was the girls' hostel entrance and I had to leave her hand.

I felt that day, when you start caring for someone more than yourself, the world calls it love, but I would define it as my life. While I was in the bus returning to my room, I wrote a text message to her- "Wish I could go inside your hostel holding your hand and sit beside you. I am sure you would recover soon. Take care, my *Babyjaan......*"

This is what I said during the fifth semester, after spending two and half years with her, and I meant it! Since she was unwell, so she did not reply...

Our telephonic studies continued and in the 5th semester, I scored eighty two percent. That year she was the topper with eighty nine percent. I was happy for her and she was for me, since I was gradually doing better. Those monthly outings were more like dates for us… watching Mamma-Mia on the last seat with four people in the entire multiplex, playing in the sea water at Marina beach was among our favorite activities of our outings!!!

During our sixth semester, Aastha's parents visited Chennai. They had to go for a regular health check up of her father at Apollo who was in his early 50's. As I was in touch with everyone from her family, I was with them from the day he was admitted till they left Chennai.

I moved from ATM to medical stores, and stood beside Aastha and supported aunty all the while. His tests were conducted by end of the day. I was about to leave for my room but something within me, made me say that evening- "Aunty I would stay with uncle here, you and Aastha take rest at the hotel since only one attendant is allowed to stay in the hospital during night." She agreed to it since whoso ever stayed at the hospital, one would have to be alone in the Hotel. That night I was with her father taking care of every small thing. Even when he was changed his side on the bed, I didn't miss to ask him if he was fine and accompanied him whenever he had to go to the washroom.

Frankly speaking I had never done anything like that for my parents till then, but being with her Dad made me feel that he was my Dad, not hers. I have always respected him. The next morning, the doctor came with the report. Aastha and her Mom had arrived by that time. Doctor asked Aastha and me to come to her chamber. As we entered her chamber, she said "Look, the blood report, X-Ray report everything are normal but…" Aastha interrupted, "What do you mean by but doctor?"

She said, "You need to take a quick decision."

"Quick decision?" I asked astonished.

The doctor asked us to calm down and showed us the reports. Being students of Engineering, we could not understand much. Aastha was impatient by then. Frantically she shouted at doctor, "Would you please let us know, what do you mean by quick decision?" I seized Aastha's hand to listen to the doctor's reply. She said, "Your father has three major and two minor blocks in the arteries, which have to be operated immediately. The expense would be around two Lac rupees"

I know it may not be a huge amount for many, but for a family whose only source of income is the father, it did mean a lot. I could see tears rolling out of her eyes. How I wished to stop them, bring the money to the doctor and ask her to go ahead with the treatment. That instant when she cried and held me close in front of the doctor, I realized my importance and what I had become for her. I really wished I could spin a magic wand to erase her pain and problems.

Waiting in the cabin with uncle, aunty was of unaware of this fact. As we came back to the cabin, aunty anxiously asked us a countless number of questions, "What did the doctor say? Is everything fine? When will he be discharged?" I took her outside the room and explained to her everything. I added, "God is with us, don't worry aunty." I have seen many strong ladies before but talking to her that day and seeing her reaction made me meet one more! She didn't cry. Rather she said, "We have been struggling for many things since a long time. This is yet another challenge to face!" and she went inside the cabin.

I was quite surprised the way she handled the situation and I got to know how Aastha had become so strong. Post a lot of discussions among themselves, they decided to go ahead with the operation at Apollo but in Kolkata instead of Chennai, since it is always good if your home is close by the hospital. This avoids travelling after surgery. By-pass surgery is common these days, but was serious and crucial for her family. So uncle and aunty returned to Kolkata to fix an appointment for the surgery. It took seven days for them to finalize the date. Aastha was supposed to be there, but how could I leave her alone. I decided to be with her and somehow managed to convince my parents, as always.

By God's grace, everything went well and we returned within ten days. While returning, something happened which I never thought would happen so early. She said, "Bawarchi I feel the same for you what you feel about me." I understood what she meant to say but behaved as if I did not get her point, just to hear it once more from her. When I asked "What do you mean by that?" she replied, "Some things are meant to be understood, instead of repeating." The girl, who looked as hard as a stone from outside, who was so arrogant to the rest of world, also carried such a pure heart and I had conquered my place there!! It felt as if I had won the world, as if I was in the seventh heaven, as if I was on the cloud nine!!!

The time I had spent with her shopping, studying and romancing over the phone suddenly flashed in my mind and I realized how it felt when you love someone and get it back. That was how the sixth semester ended.

July 2008, our campus placement had begun. It was the time when the market was affected by recession quite horribly. Since I was the student placement co-ordinator, my Dean placement had a lot of expectation from me. Satyam was the first company that came for the campus, but both of us were not even able to clear the first round. We were disappointed, so was my Dean.

A month later, another campus interview was arranged for us, which was an IT-MNC. That time I was not allowed to appear for the campus placement drive since the company was looking for students with seventy percent throughout without a year gap.

I had spent a year in Delhi for IIT preparations. So I could not appear for the placement. But I was happy since Aastha was eligible and I had a hope that she would definitely clear the campus interview. While I wasn't able to get into that IT firm, she too denied going for the campus drive. I tried to convince her not to leave the opportunity, and take it as if we were going for a movie.

After a lot of persuasion that night, I induced her for the campus interview.

 It was Second week of August;

I was allowed to be there during the process since I was the co-coordinator. I was with her throughout the session till evening, when I saw her running towards me. She hugged me and said, "I won the Oscar." I was happy; my last night's efforts did give her the prize, the prize she very much deserved. Only two from our college were selected for that company. We parted that evening.

The country was hit with recession, so many companies refused to visit the campus, but with efforts of our college we got the next MNC in the month of October. 23rd October 2008; I appeared for the company and cleared the written, technical and even HR round. My offer letter was in my hand

and happiness on my face. I went to the Dean's room to share it with her. She was equally happy for me.

My happiness knew no bounds and I called everybody - my Dad, Mom, sister, brother and friends to share my life's best feeling after getting a job. Both of us were placed now, but she was supposed to join Chennai and I had to report to Bangalore. But when? That would be intimated later. At least we would be close to each other, was one of the reasons of our happiness. We planned to come every weekend to Bangalore and Chennai alternatively, since it was just overnight journey.

We were on the verge to begin with the last semester. As always, we were together, while going and coming back from our home towns to college which was many times objected by my family. Sometimes by hiding the truth, sometimes by lying, we continued being together till last day in college.

This last semester was started with two surprises -

First one, which I had never dreamt nor thought but that was the truth- I was the college topper in the seventh semester with a round off ninety percent. It was a miracle for me or I would say it was her efforts, dedication and love which made me reach the top! I did it, I did it for her. A guy who had thought seventy percent was enough to clear the degree, proudly scored ninety percent. It was an amazing feeling as she was the second topper with eighty eight percent. Wishes and congratulations flowed in and we celebrated that day like never before. Those late night studies, those telephonic studies had done the trick for us.

And the second surprise was she had successfully convinced her parents to allow her to stay in a PG accommodation at Kelambakkam, close to where I was staying. She had become my neighbor of the next street. Luck seemed to favor us, God was blessing us like never before. Going for morning walk, traveling together, dining for at restaurants had become a regular habit. The only thing which was killing us within was the fact that we hardly had three to four months before the college would end. I used to cook a variety of dishes along with Vinit and share the dishes with her to her PG. I was justifying my name Bawarchi and she was justifying hers... my *Babyjaan*!!!!

College Trip to Yelagiri

C03

Our college had announced a trip to Yelagiri. As we had never got such an opportunity to come together with students of other departments outside college, so it was the best time to do so before we'd say good bye to our college. We were excited for this opportunity wherein we would be able to interact with other students from various departments. I hadn't heard of but Yelagiri before. How this place would be, probably no one had any idea.

We assembled at the canteen to discuss about our plans for the trip. We had to pay fifteen hundred rupees 1500 per head and rest of the things would be arranged by the college. The trip was for three nights and two days to Yelagiri and it was not mandatory for all students. Those interested to go for the trip, had to register their names by next week; informed the Bio-medical Department HOD who was very keen in arranging such activities. So this meeting among us was important. We had two weeks to stay in college before our final semester was scheduled to begin. So being a part of this trip was a great idea.

Post lunch, we eight members of our group met in the canteen bunking our classes. We were trying to find out the possible way to ask for money from our parents. Raj suddenly said- "Hey guys we have to buy our books."

"Books?" everyone was surprised.

Raj continued, "Yes, books for this semester project which

will cost around fifteen hundred rupees .This is what exactly we can tell our parents and this is how we will be able to get the fund. What do you think guys?"

"The idea is great but what if we have to spend again something for this project just after returning from this trip," asked Jassi?

I was good in getting info from all the places. I supported Raj by saying "Guys don't worry. I know a place beside Chennai Central named Moore Market where we can get second hand readymade project books in half the price. If need be, we can ask for more money from our parents later." The idea of Raj supported by mine was appreciated by everyone and we decided at the meeting that we would definitely go for the trip. So that night almost each one of us talked to their parents about this newly innovative idea for the much needed fund. But I was sure even if we had shared the truth with our parents they would have agreed. Yet who wants to take risk.

The same night, we received calls from our group's girls, who were anxious to know whether or not we were going. Most of the girls were sure that their parents might not allow them for the trip. And since there were few months left till completing their degree, they did not want to argue with their parents. Anyway I wanted my Aastha to go for this trip but taking her alone in this trip would not have been be a good idea unless few others girls were ready for this trip. I was positive that from other department girls would definitely join us for the trip, but wasn't sure about girls from my own department. So I did not request Aastha to be with me.

Aastha and I had discussed, fought and then smiled over this issue. Finally the last day to submit the money arrived. We eight friends and other boys assembled at Bio-Medical HOD's room to register the names and submit the money. She asked us to form a queue, parallel to the girls' queue. To my surprise I saw Aastha and eight other girls from our department. Aastha had managed to motivate others and the result was in front of me. I was happy and so was Abhi because by then he secretly loved a girl of our department.

Sumit always shifted his focus to the most beautiful girl. We were happy to see his dream girl going for this trip. There was a girl named Sakshi in our department who was damn pretty and the way she used to carry herself was remarkable. I was quite sure that some eighty five percent of the guys in my department were crazy for her. Undoubtedly, most of the secret lovers were indeed overjoyed to see Sakshi joining us for the trip. The next week passed in planning fun for the tour. Three nights and two days were enough for a bundle of mischief and entertainment. There were diverse questions like where would the girls stay, whether they stay with us, who was the faculty members going with us and so on ...

These questions kept haunting our minds and the week passed away till the final day for the trip. It was a Friday and we were asked to assemble at the college campus at 8:30 pm. We had done some research already and found that Yelagiri was about two hundred and fifty kilometers from our college which would take a maximum of five hours to reach there. The place was famous as a hill station which had paragliding as the main attraction. Our group assembled at 8:10 pm at college canteen. Four buses were waiting in queue one after another with banners on each bus. The buses did look good, at least from outside.

Sharp at 8:30 pm, eight of our faculty members gathered in front of our bus and asked us to get board the bus. On seeing our department's favorite teachers in the group, added to our happiness. It was the girls' turn to get inside the bus. We boys tried to act smart enough to occupy the front seat prior to the girls but our smartness got dejected by our favorite faculty when she asked the girls to take seats in the front.

Tilak exclaimed "We don't have a problem if girls sit beside us." We all laughed but had to vacate the seats. Women reservation on such a day was not fair, yet we had to accept the position without a choice. All the buses started somewhere around 9:30pm post cross checking the entry of all students .There was capacity of fifty people in 2 X 2 push back seats. We began our exciting journey followed by the unique hooting which we did while entering the college campus on day one, "OOOOOO!!"….. and everyone followed. The spirit and enthusiasm of all our friends was visible on each one's face .We had two faculty members sitting with us in our bus and they were our favorite faculties. Gradually their restraint changed and we hovered around the faculty members for songs and fun activities. We decided to start with truth and dare.

The bus had all department students; CS/Mechanical/EEE/ ETC/ECE and few others. While everyone was busy with singing songs and dancing in bus, Aastha and I had captured the backseat. We began talking. Words flowed in such a way within few minutes we forgot that we were in a bus with our groups. It was an air conditioned bus so the temperature was pretty cool inside, but I guess the noise and uproar with every ending song was escalating the temperature inside. While we were indulged in talking to each other, all of a sudden our group was in front of us, teasing us like anything. Someone among them commented- "Hello, this is not a couple trip, it's a group trip" and others had a hearty laugh.

I wished I could be with Aastha but I too realized it was a group trip. There were fifteen other girls and rest were boys in the bus. We then decided to join the group singing and dancing. Around half past midnight, our bus halted at Vellore Highway beside a Dhaba, and all three buses followed. The well lighted Dhaba looked wonderful in the midnight. It was then time to respond to nature's call. There was a long queue at girl's side while boys were through within no time. Who cares once below the sky in the field :)

While the natural process was going on, Sumit commented, "Guys, I have heard that you cannot do anything like this in foreign countries." We all laughed at that statement and said- "We love our India."

I munched on snacks, others got busy in buying stock of cigarettes while others were bought bottles of cold drinks. Again after thirty minutes of halt, the bus resumed its journey at 1:00 am. After being fully refreshed, we continued to sing, tease, pulling legs and everything to make others happy. Soon, after an hour, few started feeling exhausted and slept instantly. But there was no weariness in Aastha's and my eyes. Nevertheless we thought it'd be better to take rest so that we could enjoy next day.

It was almost morning when I opened my eyes and found Aastha sleeping on my shoulder. We have reached somewhere close to our destination.

"Hey guys get up. We have reached Yelagiri. Everybody please get down," said a Prof.

Few among us were struggling hard to open their eyes. The cool breeze and a pleasant sunrise had made the place more beautiful. All two hundred of us were waiting for the next move.

The crowd was addressed by one of the faculty members – "Listen everybody; we have the rooms booked with triple occupancy," pointing towards a hotel. "So you all need to get yourself settled with two other room mates. All girls would occupy the ground floor and boys need to occupy the first, second, and third floors. Please make sure you all assemble here after three hours by 8:00 am max. We will go for trekking."

We rushed competing with others to occupy the best room. It reminded me of the day once again when we had to run to occupy our rooms in the hostel. All of us managed to get into our room and Jassi, Sumit and I decided to stay together. We prepared ourselves for the adventurous trekking. All boys and girls were ready like athletes by 8:00 am.

"We will proceed to Swamimalai which is at a stretch of four kilometers. We'll cover the distance mounting the hills. But before we begin, that we will have some breakfast," said our teacher. Breakfast was quite fascinating. A buffet was laid for us. Everyone hogged above their limits without keeping it in mind the fact that had to climbing up the hills! I wouldn't blame them, since human beings don't let go opportunity of over eating when served in a party or when the food is sponsored. As expected the breakfast exceeded the time limit since everyone needed time to digest that heavy intake. To my surprise girls were not feeling uncomfortable unlike boys.

But when it was time to climb the hills, girls quitted one after the other. It wasn't surprising to see girls vomiting at every 20 steps. Scaling the four thousand three hundred and thirty eight feet rock was not an easy task. Guys from the mechanical department quick to climb and we were followed them. There were many love birds in the group including Aastha and me.

After two hours of climbing the hills, we reached mid way and decided to take some rest. While everyone was busy in taking rest, few guys from Bio-tech department clicked pictures. One of the guys named Anuj posed for the camera with his one leg on a rock and another one at against a tree. To our surprise that little weak tree gave way and he started rolling down, through the rock and stones.

From that height we could do anything but shout. We watched him holding our breath, rolling down thousand feet. He hurt himself quite badly. We all were about to run and help him but our faculties asked us not to go in group, else somebody might slip again. Few boys and two faculty members reached him. What actually happened, we could only partially witness from the top. After fifty minutes or so, we saw Anuj accompanied by three boys mounting up the hills. The point where we had halted offered a breathtaking view of the valleys. But nobody could enjoy the beauty of that place after the ugly incident.

When he came up, we saw Anuj badly injured in various place. He was bleeding from many places besides the minor injuries of his body. He was given immediate first aid and we started the journey again with the enthusiasm and confidence, learning from Anuj. Everyone got over conscious and extremely careful about rock climbing. Crossing through the bushes and stone was exciting but that adventurous trip was successful when we reached the top from where the entire valley was visible. It was spectacular to watch the whole region from that height.

We clicked several pictures with our group. As we were late to reach the hill top, we were asked to get down the hills as soon as possible before it got dark. After spending an hour or so there, we started for the return journey from the valley. As we had our hotel booked, we safely entered the hotel rooms without worrying about snakes or insects or other nocturnal creatures of the hills. By God's grace nothing unexpected happened while coming down.

Everyone was hungry and tired at the same time. Washrooms were flooded with people to take shower. By 8:30 pm we gathered for dinner, again served in buffet. Food was excellent and hungry as always, we ate more. After the dinner, lot of games and activities had been planned for us. We began with musical chair and Antakhshari. Love birds again got some time to spend together.

After some time, Aastha noticed Sumit missing along with Nikshita, a girl from the Biotech department. We didn't know whether the same had been noticed by others or not since everyone was busy in activities. Abruptly Aastha asked for permission from a faculty to go to the hotel room for a medicine. The faculty was well aware of our relation by that time; in fact whole college knew about our association, so she asked me to go along with her.

While going with her we both thought where Sumit had disappeared so stupidly. We also knew that Nikshita had a limited interaction with Sumit till date. Were they together somewhere? With these thoughts in our mind, we came to Aastha's room. Never before I had entered any girl's room so was unable to keep myself calm. I told Aastha – "Let's search Sumit." As our room's key was with me, so there was no point in Sumit staying in our room. Then where had the stupid Sumit gone??? Suddenly, she stopped me saying "Look at that door. There is no lock hanging outside. It has been locked from inside."

"Yes!" I exclaimed with excitement. When we came closer to the room, she was right, the room was locked from inside. Was that Sumit inside with Nikshita? Were they doing something??? All these questions were running in my as well as Aastha's mind. But how do we get to know this? There was to peep inside the room from outside.

"Shhh. Listen, I can hear them talking," I said to Aastha. She tapped me on my head saying "It's the sound of TV." I knew Sumit was not a fool but I couldn't stay there long as a detective or else Aastha would have kicked me. So I had left the place with her, otherwise I would have managed to be the witness of the live telecast. We went back and joined the crowd, enjoying to the fullest.

Thirty minutes later, we noticed Nikshita coming towards the group from the hotel area but Sumit was not there. She came and sat there and got her so much involved as if she was with the group from a long time. After fifteen minutes, I was surprised to see sumit coming from the same side arranging his hair. He sat next to me and started playing antakshiri. I looked at his face to find out if anything was wrong but dear Sumit was smart enough not to show that in his face. The best part in my friendship with him was he had never hidden anything from me. So I was sure once this activity ended, he would tell me the truth. The musical programme continued till 2:00am and we retired to our rooms to sleep.

As Jassi, Sumit and I entered the room and closed the door, we fired a volley of questions at Sumit. The first question came from my side, "What the hell did you do with Nikshita?

He was about to answer when all of a sudden someone knocked at the door. "Someone at 2am?" said Jassi and went to open the door.

"All those who want to booze, come to the top floor." Jassi and I nodded our heads. Sumit asked us to shut the door and sleep as he was well aware that we don't booze. Jassi and I kept imagining what possibly might have happened between the two. We slept while discussing the possibilities.

Next morning when I woke up, it was already fifteen minutes past nine. " Ohhhh shit we will miss Jalagamparai waterfalls trip. Guys get ready."

It looked like Sumit had a strong drink as he had spent the night sleeping on floor, till I woke up .The reporting time was 11:00 am. The murmuring Attaru River flows through the Yelagiri Hills, and plummets down to form a highly captivating waterfall. It is an hour; five kilometers walk from Yelagiri downhill. Though there was a direct route from Yelagiri to the fall but it was often closed. One had to go all the way down the hill, take the plains, and then climb the hill on the other side. It's an hour's journey. So after a light breakfast that day we reached Jalagamparai waterfall at 12:30 pm.

The Boys were super excited. At the same time it was difficult for them to believe that they would have a bath in the waterfall with girls together! All of us knew how wild we actually were and to which extend we could go. It was unimaginable! The waterfall fun was superb; taking bath in chilled water in such a wonderful atmosphere was rare and truly awesome. We had almost forgotten to ask Sumit about his last night experience. Jassi and I along with everyone else soaked ourselves in the water under the sun. I wished the fun never ended. After spending three hours, we came out of water. For boys it was easy to change but for girls it was impossible. They were worried and we were anxious to know what they were going to do next. I was concerned about Aastha but that day we both decided to enjoy with the group. Soon, a temporary changing room was built with the help of tent cloth and all girls one by one changed into dry clothes.

By evening we returned to our room again and we determined to hear Sumit's story then. Everything was ready and Sumit was about to start with his story, that someone again knocked the door. I said – " Oh no, again a drink. Sumit, please tell us." He rushed towards door. It was one of the faculty members who took Sumit outside the room. We followed him. The faculty took Sumit to the ground floor and started walking towards Nikshita's Room.

"Oh no! What happened? Anything serious?" exclaimed Jassi.

Something had definitely gone wrong.

"Did they get caught or is she pregnant?" I spoke out loud.

Jassi kicked my ass saying, "Come on. No one gets to know about pregnancy overnight."

But then why did the faculty take him? They both entered a room and locked it from inside. We could not judge what was going on. I could sense something terribly wrong. We thought it wasn't good to stand in front of a girl's room, so we went back to our room.

There was poor network connectivity; hence we could not call anybody. After an hour Sumit came back to our room. He was totally silent for few minutes. We pestered him to speak out, and when he did, he got a 440 watt shock.

Sumit and Nikshita were in love with each other from the past six months. They used to talk for hours over the phone, shared each and everything and romanced over the phone. Last night when they got an opportunity, they turned all those telephonic fantasy to reality. Today after returning from the waterfall trip, she tried to commit suicide by slitting her wrist. One of the professors had noticed the mishap while passing by and called Sumit to her room.

"You were in love from the past six months and you f*ck*r, you didn't even bother to tell us. And why did she try to kill herself?"

We had endless questions but Sumit had no answer for anything except a reply which didn't give us guts to ask him anything further. He said, "I had truly loved her for the last six months yaar but I could not take it when I heard last night while I was in bed with her that she was in a relationship with a boy from four years. I lost my mind and slapped her. I asked her to go away from my life. She has ditched me and I just wanted her to be away from my life."

He was feeling bad and thinking whom to blame. We too felt awful. One cannot measure the degree of love, no matter what, and it was his true love. Before meeting everyone in the at the hotel lawn we thought to meet Nikshita. Her wrist was bandaged. We could not say anything except "Take care." We had no words to comfort her or advice her, though we knew the story behind it.

It was the last night of our trip before we started at 11:30 pm. We met at 7:00 pm in the hotel lawn to discuss about various inputs and outputs from individuals. There was a common question asked to everyone, "If god gives you another chance to spend college life, one thing you would like to do?" Everyone came up with numerous answers, few humorous, few serious, few were touchy but Nikshita's reply was enough, at least and Jassi and I, to know what happened last night with Sumit. Trying hard to hide her tears, she replied "Making someone realize that you were not my lust." Everyone clapped on her answer. Few girls started asking her questions but only Jassi, Aastha and I could understand for whom this reply was meant. But he too was right at his point. Few people get closer in life but it's hard to find the reason behind it. May be this was the same for Sumit and Nikshita, I concluded mentally. With that farewell note and after dinner we started for our college. On the way back I sat with Aastha, as everyone was tired and sleepy. This trip to Yelagiri had certainly created evergreen memories in everybody's heart, but for Nikshita it was more than a memory.

Last Day Of college!!!

 CB

After that wonderful team outing we were back to our college and only few days were left in the college, where we had spent four memorable years of our life. We all were heartbroken with the thought that the beautiful journey would come to end within few days. In our last semester, we had to write two theory papers and one project.

Due to recession, only few companies had visited our campus but still there were some lucky guys (including me) who got the offer from some company or the other, yet the joining date was uncertain. Appearing for the last two theory papers' examination was not difficult for us and I believe most of us were busy in counting the days left with us

Ten days to go, Nine days to go and so on….

During those days, I felt twenty four hours in a day were too less to spend time with Aastha, Vinit and all my other batch mates. I wanted to spend time with my juniors like Sarwesh, Deepanjan, Anirudh, Poulomi and few others who had always treated me like their elder brother. But to manage time with all of them was pretty hard. For those last few days, most of us were staying in Kelambakkam, so we used to go for morning walk together.

Aastha and Poulomi used to join us from their PG and rest of us assembled at the main street close to girl's PG. Deepanjan being the naughtiest junior, never missed a chance to comment that made us giggle nonstop. Sometimes we had to leave the place where we used to wait for the girls. Aastha used to enjoy Deepanjan's hilarious jokes.

Everyone in our group including juniors knew about our relationship. They used to say the same thing every time we met "Don't forget to invite us to your marriage." At times they used to calculate the number of years we would get married in, according to them.

While those discussions were in full swing among juniors, Aastha used to look at me and we used to smile looking at each other. Our classes were suspended for preparatory leaves ten days before our theory exams. However, for us it was like spending time with near and dear ones. I presume this was the only semester when we didn't open our book even before a week of exam. Earlier to this Aastha always had insisted and forced me to study. Fortunately my good scores were the outcome of her pressure. I still remember during those days, when not even a single day passed without Vinit, Aastha and I having ice cream in an Ice-cream parlor every evening. Pouncing on the ice cream tubs and fighting for large scoops with spoons, still brings a smile to my face. We were really enjoying those moments.

Days moved on smoothly with a recurring thought in mind, that "Tomorrow we may have to say that this is our last day of college." Exams began; there was a gap of three days between each paper. We wrote our first quite well and we were back to prepare for the last paper of the Engineering degree. Fifty Six exams all together out of which forty were theory exams one after another, indeed was not an easy task. It was believed among us, that if you don't have arrears (re-exam) you cannot claim yourself to be an Engineer. Unfortunately Aastha's motivation to study hard had never given me a chance to experience that, but it was good to see myself as an Engineer without arrears.

It was 5ᵗʰ May 2009. I along with other friends of our batch were getting ready for the college for the last time as I was sure hereafter there would be no struggle in the morning to get into bus number 212, 115 or 515, there would be any formal dress, no assignment to be made, no more exams, as that day was supposed to be the last exam for all to get an Engineering degree. There was a mixed feeling among us; the good one was for – "Hurray!!! No more exams" ☺ but bad feeling was "Ohhhh nooooo!!! No more exams?" ☹

Appearing in exams is fun in itself as most of the students pray hard not to get front seats. Looking at the seating arrangement, few try to reach as early as possible to write few answers on desk. The best practice was done by few of the experts in this domain, who used to keep micro xerox inside socks. Incredible engineers!

Suveet, whose registration number was close to mine, always used to get a seat beside or behind me; and my responsibility was to inform him about the specific chapter from where the question was asked, so that he could take out the micro xerox copies from his socks, which he used to keep in the order of the chapters. Sometimes his micro xeroxes were also useful for me, provided they were in bigger fonts. I often wondered how he even managed to see anything on the miniature size papers with microscopic fonts! I was going to miss all this badly and was sure that everybody else would too.

The exam began at its scheduled time sharp 10:00 am. While writing the answers on the answer sheets, I thought- "Another three hours left and it will be all over. I would be recognized as an Engineer like five hundred other Engineers from various departments in my college." At 12:30 pm, a notice was circulated to each and every examination hall. As the peon entered our hall, we all shouted in a sync "Oooooo!!" without knowing the reason. Our TLN Mam shouted at us and asked us to assemble in the auditorium after exam. On asking her the reason, she replied that the crowd would be address by our principal. But the agenda was not mentioned in the notice.

On hearing this, the hall was full of murmuring and whispers breaking the silence once again. As expected, it was interrupted by the high pitch tone of our TLN Mam "Stopppppppppppppppp."

Everybody raced to finish their papers. Few of them finished early and left. I was in a hurry to complete, as by that time I had incorporated a habit of writing a lot with good presentation. My batch mates Tuhin and Simant used to taunt me "Ab ho gaya" (It is enough now-save paper save earth).

As we all completed the paper, we walked towards the auditorium and like every year after exams ended, Aastha was waiting for me. As I reached close to her, she asked me how I had written the paper. I didn't comprehend what made her so sincere that instead of asking about the meeting she was discussing the question paper. I put my hand on her shoulder and said, "*Babyjaan* it's over now. Let's go and find out what's special for us today in auditorium."

She folded her question paper, shoved it in her bag and followed me to the to the auditorium gate. The gate was closed and progressively all five hundred students of final year, rather final day, students gathered there. The gate was thrown open to us all of a sudden and we were thrown a pleasant surprise by our juniors. They had arranged a get together for us. We had never done anything like that for our seniors.

Each and every thing in the auditorium, be it the stage, the walls, the chairs, was well decorated. Looking at that, one could easily judge the efforts our juniors had put in for us. As our principal Mam, heads of the departments and faculties entered the auditorium, we stood up. By then the auditorium was packed with five hundred final day students, around hundred juniors and hundred faculty staff members. Principal and HODs took their seats on the stage and the anchoring was done by Sanjeev and Pushpam (two great voices among our juniors).We were overwhelmed by this gesture of our juniors. One by one, emotional and valuable speeches were delivered by our Principal and HODs. Each and every sentence they spoke that day seemed right and valuable.

In the last four years, whenever they had said anything, everyone had tried to ignore, and whenever I was into the dice I had to keep nodding my head even if I was in disagreement with their statement. But trust, me that day everything was coming excellent. The speech from Electronics Department HOD made everyone emotional. I found my eyes welled up too! It's true whatever feeling you hold for a system or someone, when the time comes to say good bye, you suddenly start loving the system and then you start missing the moments spent. Same was happening with us.

After the thirty minutes speech we were astounded to watch a video which had been recorded by our juniors as a sting operation somewhere in the exam hall or washroom or even in the hostel. It was fun to look at your own video on that day. The video showed us teasing girls, the fights we had while conquering the washroom and so on. The examination hall scene was remarkable to view. Each one of us was thankful to our juniors and college management for making our last day in the college so memorable.

One by one, students were pulled out to say few words, share experiences, and the hard and soft feelings. I don't know how, but that day, saying all hard truth for someone was also good to hear. Even saying something about faculty members or principal Mam, was so easy that day because of the environment created by our juniors. It was like disposing all the hard feelings we had any for the college, before we left.

Stage performances followed with mimicking our batch mates and relishing snacks. This platform was highly appreciated because during snacks, we friends also interacted with each other apologizing for the little silly things that might have hurt them.

It was really good to watch few boys apologizing to the girls for the teasing or the stupid proposal they had made, and for few guys who got the positive reply of their proposals, like me, became the center of attraction. We did enjoy that day a lot. Everyone in our batch was presented with a memento of lord Vinayaka which symbolizes memory and wishes for future.

None of us could control our tears when it was announced to say good byes. Staying away from home was tough but during those four years we had built a home among ourselves and to leave that home was tough job. Nobody knew where life would take us as none of us had got any joining confirmation from the firms till that date.

Wiping tears from our eyes and cherishing memories in our hearts, we headed for Kelambakkam. Aastha and my group were with me and we had not yet bid good bye to each other. The last day of college took us back to our old days. The day we had stepped into the college, few of us cried as we had to be away from home but that day everyone cried as we were stepping out of the main gate leaving behind our college ,our second home where we have spent the most beautiful part of our lives;, where I got the most awaited gift of my life Aastha, where I got the most delightful friend of my life and above all where I fulfilled my dreams with the most desired label my Dad always wanted to listen- An Engineer. But I had to leave those golden memories behind on the last day of my college.

That Trip with her to the city of Salem

୯୫

I term this as my first long journey alone with her, but eventually it turned out to be an experience which I could have never imagined to be so exciting.

That was not a planned trip. It happened under unavoidable circumstances.

Our final semester had ended two months ago; we went back for few days to our home but returned to the hostel soon. We both had planned to stay till our results were declared. Our college used to take forty five days to hand over the degrees to the students. Since many of us were waiting desperately for the final degree for which all of us had spent four years, with sleepless nights, dedicated studies at late nights during semester exams and many memories in between them. It was 4th June 2009; we came to know that we had to collect our final degree from our university, located in Salem-a stainless steel producing city. Salem was an overnight journey from Chennai. The transport facilities in Tamil Nadu are among the best as compared to other cities I have come across till date.

So, Aastha (*Babyjaan*) and I planned to begin our journey in late evening to reach the steel city Salem in the morning.

The PG where *Babyjaan* stayed had no strict regulations unlike our college hostel. We started around 6:30 pm to CMBT bus terminal which was an hour's journey from Kelambakkam.

We reached there within an hour and had our dinner at Ananda Bhavan (One of the best and most reasonable restaurants in Tamil Nadu). Post dinner we came back to the bus terminal to start for the most memorable journey.

One has the option to choose among the Volvo, deluxe, semi deluxe or sleeper buses and the bus frequency was every thirty minutes. We boarded a pink color TNSTC Volvo bus. Luckily we both got the last seat. It was a bumpy ride but every young couple like us looks for the last seat in a theatre or during a bus journey. There is something interesting in the last seat.

The bus started its usual journey, but a special one for me at 9:45 pm. That was the first time after four years that my *Babyjaan* and I would stay together for the next twenty four hours or so. Usually these journeys used to happen after every six months during our semester break, but those were train journeys, quite different from overnight bus journey. We have been accompanied by our college mates each time unlike that day when Aastha and I were alone.

The bus reached the highway after a drive of forty five minutes. Most of the passengers had either slept or were ready to sleep. For me, I felt out of the world, sitting so close to her for the first time.

Babyjaan, as usual started asking what should we do after going home- wait for the companies' joining date or try searching another job or go for higher studies?

She spoke continuously while I simply nodded my head. The vehicles on the road coming from the opposite side illuminated her eyes and lips. I was spell bound.

Aastha was a natural beauty by her looks. And that day, she appeared to me as the most beautiful girl in the world. After every sentence she finished, I asked her, "Do you want to say anything to me?" and every time she replied the same thing, "So whom am I saying all this to?"

Her deep black eyes with pinkish face were so beautiful to watch that I couldn't blink my eyes. The weather was turning cold as the night progressed. We wrapped ourselves in a warm bed- spread, with our faces peeping outside. I soon found *Babyjaan* holding my hand. That earnest feeling was so exciting that I felt like hugging her, may be because the moment was special. It had never happened to me before. She placed her head on my shoulder and our hands were locked. That blissful moment, I felt something extremely different. I realized, she was my responsibility and she had trusted me more than anybody else in the world.

I wish I could have captured those lovely moments of togetherness in my camera at least but those days I used to have a Nokia 1100-considered to be an ideal phone for student life.

The chit chat went on for hours. It was midnight by then. I could see that less number of vehicles plying on the roads. I thought *Babyjaan* had slept on my shoulder but suddenly some one whispered in my ear saying "Will you marry me?"

I could not find anybody around to say that. I was speechless. Where did that question come from? Since I thought *Babyjaan* had slept, I too was about to sleep. The same voice and the same words came to my ears again "Will you marry me?" I again checked whether it was what I wanted to hear from her again or it was my imagination or was it she who said that. Those words did not come again when I was attentive but I realized may be it was just a dream. I looked at her and found she was sleeping. I sat still and became alert again to know how could a voice so clear be merely a dream? Just then someone whispered again "Will …?" I quickly opened my eyes and found she was murmuring. I interrupted her saying "Can I marry you now?" Both of us laughed, smiled and hugged and she just said one thing "Please don't go away even if you find somebody better than me" before our first ever kiss. We were soon distracted by that shouting conductor when he said something in Tamil; I figured it out that it was a mid-way halt.

After a break of twenty minutes, the bus started again at 12:45 am for the rest of the journey. I could not stop abusing the silly conductor, " *Saale ko yaahin rukna tha.* " (Why did the stupid guy halt here?) We resumed with the journey and other co-passengers took their time to settle down. By 2:00 am the passengers had slept and the bus was calm, exactly how it was before the half way break.

When you are with your love, time actually flies and you don't even feel it. We kept discussing about our future and we were not able to come up with a single conclusion what to do next after going home.

Around 3:00am, we decided to sleep for few hours before getting down the bus. Her head rested on my shoulder, our hands locked and we both sat inside a blanket till the bus finally reached Salem. Morning 5:00 am we reached the destination. It was quite cold and all passengers had vacated the bus. I tried to wake her up, "Hey *Babyjaan* we have reached." She managed to rouse soon and we got down at the Salem bus stop. I have always considered that travel in a bus is always good; at least you are sure some one will shout once the bus reaches the final destination while in contrast to a train, you may end up waking up at the yard after reaching the final destination.

The birds chirped around, the day was about to begin with the first sunrays ready to come out in the sky. I had thought of booking a hotel but later decided to head straightaway to the University since by the end of the day, we were required to have all certificates in our hand; be it migration, provisional certificate or consolidated marks sheet. We had heard from other friends that they hardly gave the documents in one day. So to make it sure, we thought to reach by 8 am; an hour before the scheduled office timing. We freshened up at the waiting room of the bus stop and had our breakfast comprising Poori Sabzi and Pongal. We boarded a bus to reach Aaiyanoor where the University head-office was located. After awaiting our turn for an hour, we were first in the queue to apply for our certificates.

By the time the counter was thrown open for public, we were glad and quite satisfied to see around hundred students standing in queue to collect their certificates, all behind us. A visible sense of satisfaction was visible on our face. However our contentment proved to be a waste when a peon arrived with a notice stating "This counter will remain closed today and the certificates will be issued from the next building's room number 34." There was a commotion around with a marathon among all students. Few people, even before reading the notice started running, since others always believe in following others.

The situation was such; it seemed that the one who would find the shortest route to the counter would reach fastest. Somehow Aastha and I both managed to reach the counter. We were fifth in the queue by then. From first to the fifth position, not a bad performance it was! Thanks to *Babyjaan* who was quite a fast runner.

We applied for the certificate at half past nine. We both, in-fact she was more worried whether or not we would be able to get our certificates by end of the day. Every hour passed with the same question in our minds, whether our certificates would be given to us or not.

The two hundred students in the queue submitted their forms to receive those valuable degrees; few of them were like us who wanted to get it before the end of the day. Amidst the confusion, the lunch break started. We went to the University canteen to eat something. I was calm and mentally preparing myself just in case we did not get our certificates that day. But she was worried and somehow positive to get those certificates the same day.

After lunch we met the concerned person and requested him to issue the certificate as early as possible, since we had to return to Chennai; and she being a girl could not during night alone. He assured us that he would try his best and asked us to check by five in the evening. It was 3 pm. then and we were stuck with the same question whether or not we would get it by the end of the day.

Every passing minute added to our worries. Suddenly we found Shantanu, a good friend of us from the mechanical department, also there. He too had come to collect the Transcript as he got admission in a University abroad and he stayed in a guest house for that day. He offered us help saying that if in case the process got delayed, we could stay in the guest house with him.

We reminded the person about our certificates. The changing weather was quite surprising for us, from a bright sunny to a cloudy one. But we were happy to see our certificates were ready by that time. *Babyjaan* came closer to me with a content expression and mentioned that it happened all because of me, though I couldn't figure it out why the credit was given to me. Suddenly it started raining. Eventually Shantanu also got his certificate by 5:00 pm. He asked us to stay there in the guest house that night and start early the next morning when the weather got better and stopped raining.

Unkempt and without a bath since morning, we decided to accompany him to the guest house. He drove us in a rented car to the guest house. By the time we reached, we were dripping wet.

Shantanu was a person who never compromised on quality and it was evident from the guest house which he had booked for himself. The room was no less than a five star hotel, with beautiful interiors. Everything was so well nicely placed, from the kitchen ware to the flower pot at the corner of entrance. I dreamt of staying there for a couple of days but the dream was suddenly wrecked when *Babyjaan* told me "We need to get fresh as soon as possible before it starts raining heavily again." I looked outside -it was not raining anymore. Damn!

Shantanu showed us the room next to his and asked us to freshen up. I had to wait in wet clothes since Aastha was the first to conquer washroom. I was seated on a chair and impatiently waited for her to come out of the washroom. I knocked the door, shouted many times but all in vain. I fail to understand why do girls take so much time? Twenty minutes later she asked me to hand over her jeans and T-shirt from the bag. I was fuming with anger with each passing minute, since it is never a good feeling to stand in wet clothes for such a long duration. She was about to open the door and I thought of screaming at her with "What's this? Don't you have little sense that I am waiting outside for so long?" But I couldn't say anything since I froze at her sight. She emerged from the washroom in her jeans and top, trying to dry her hair with a white towel. She looked like fresh rose petals with little water drops sprinkled on them.

As she came out she said to me- "*Jao tum, jyada to wait nahi karaya na*" (You can go now. I hope I dint make you wait for long). Tight lipped I went inside the washroom.

She was right outside the washroom near the mirror, drying her hair. That mesmerizing moment flashed in front of my eyes repeatedly as I entered the washroom. I didn't want to miss the magical spectacle, so I came out of the washroom in a towel and caught her from the back in my arms. "Nahiiiiiiiiiiiiiiiiii," she shouted "*Gande bawarchi pehle naha kar aao.*" (Dirty man, take a bath first) Probably it was the magical effervescence of her voice that I hardly took ten minutes to take a bath and come out with a hope to hug her again, much tightly that time. As I came out, she was not in front of mirror. My dear friend, Shantanu had come by that time and Aastha was talking to him. I thought of that conductor and then Shantanu.

May be god was listening to my wish. By the time we were about to start for our journey, it had started raining heavily. So heavily that going to the car which was waiting outside the guest house, was not possible. We decided to wait and watch for the next thirty minutes, hoping that it may stop raining. I could see the tension on her face, but nature's wish was not in my hands.

We waited..One hour, two and three but it did not stop raining. I looked like the rain did not allow us to leave Salem that night. Till that moment, I had not thought that night would be so special in our lives. There were two rooms inside the flat, so spending a night there was not a big matter of concern for us. Frankly speaking even the washroom was so good and clean as compared to Sumit's room. It was 10:30 pm and we thought it would not be safe to travel while it was pouring heavily. Shantanu too suggested the same thing. We three decided to have our dinner together and the cook for the day was *Babyjaan*. The best part of the guest house was the availability of stuff required for cooking. The whole scenario appeared to me as if Aastha and I was married and she was cooking for a friend who had come home to visit us. Wild imagination you see! The menu for dinner was rice, *daal* and vegetable of potatoes. I asked Shantanu to take rest and offered to cook with Aastha. He agreed to the idea and couched on the sofa watching TV. I went inside the kitchen and started helping Aastha to cook. She instructed me, as if I was not aware of cooking, but she forgot to recall that in the last three years I had been cooking on my own. Nevertheless I was happy to listen to her instructions and asked her silly questions with curiosity her make her explain me more each time. And there was a suddenly power cut to which I shouted-"Shantanu light kab aayegi?" (Shantanu, when is the power expected to resume?) He replied "Soon" and left the room to check the meter outside. Aastha and I were in the kitchen at that moment. "May be this power failure would help me to hug her this time" I said to myself. It was then a hide and seeks game between me Aastha and me. I held her hand tight saying, "You cannot run out of the kitchen babu, so let's see how you can stop me from hugging you."

We enjoyed the naughtiness while trying to keep our voice as low as possible not to let Shantanu know about our game. Probably he might have heard us but he did not interfere, neither did he come to us before the power resumed. I could not see anything in the dark. It was still pouring outside. I exclaimed with joy "*Maine pakad liya,*" (I caught you) to which she replied "*Ullu woh fridge hain*" (Fool, that's the refrigerator) I checked, it was actually the fridge. "Am I so foolish?" I asked myself. But I did not mind acting like a fool if that made her smile and happy. Out of the blues, I heard a loud sound.... Dharammmmmmm as if something had fallen...I shouted for Shantanu.…...

Eventually power and Shantanu both had returned and we saw Aastha lying on the floor covering face with her palms. "Shittttt" I yelled. She had hurt her nose at the corner of the gate while she was running and that time again it was the same place where she had hurt herself when I took my "revenge." I immediately brought her to the room and made her lie down. My first aid helped to stop her bleeding. The clocked ticked 11:00 pm. Shantanu asked me if it was required to take her to the hospital. Thankfully, she was better by that time. The entire child like enjoyment suddenly turned into pain for her. We decided to have our dinner which she had cooked for us. I helped her eat while she lied on my lap. After dinner we retired to bed since we had to catch the first bus heading for Chennai. I left Aastha in the other room and slept beside Shantanu. I felt terrible as it was me who hurt her again and I was not able to sleep thinking about her pain. I kept tossing on the bed from one side to the other. Shantanu understood my condition and asked me to go to Aastha and stay with her till she slept. I was sure she would have also not slept by that time.

And I was right. As I entered her room, she said –"*Mujhe pata tha tum aaogay*" (I was sure, you will come) I sat beside her and tenderly caressed her forehead. We started talking... That night brought me much closer to her as I confessed it was me who kept that snake below her desk. I thought she would shout at me or get upset. As expected I found her angry not because I kept that snake under the desk but because I touched a dead snake! She instantly asked me to go and wash my hands. We both laughed, and laughed a lot as it was more than 3 year when

I have touched that snake and suddenly she kissed my hand. I was surprised to get a hug from her that moment. She kept her head on my shoulder. Before I could realize what happened, I felt my shoulder wet. She was crying and immediately tried to hide her tears as I saw her. She did not reply when I asked the reason behind her tears. I asked her repeatedly but she did not say a word. We both were lost somewhere in that hug….. When I opened my eyes it was already morning and we headed back for Chennai.

That Last Journey

ॐ

The trip to Salem was not even seven days ago and we had to make our last journey, even though we were waiting for our joining date, which was yet to be intimated to both of us.

Should we start preparing for higher degree in Chennai or should we go for Government job preparation or would going back home will be the best option? These discussions were common between her and I during the last fifteen days in Chennai. One fine morning we thought to settle in Chennai till we both got our joining dates but that thought never turned into reality, since we were bothered about our long term relationship for which something strong had to be decided. It was 13th June 2009, I went to Tambaram railway station to book tickets for that journey, which later became our last journey together.

Like always there was a huge rush during the morning rush hours. I was in the queue when I bumped into Wasim, one of my classmates who asked me the date of travelling. As I was not sure when would *Babyjaan* and I travel together again, I lied to him that I was booking tickets for the next week without mentioning the date though I knew it would be 19th June. I asked the same question to him to which he replied 19th.

Shocked, I asked "19th?"

"Why is there anything wrong about 19,?" asked Wasim as he passed on his form to me to book his ticket as he was not in the queue. Both my & his form were in my hands with the same date, same destination. Reluctantly I added his name to my form. As we would have huge luggage, I booked one more berth in my Dad's name. After thirty minutes, the tickets were in my hand, Dibrugarh Express, S4 seat number 3, 4, 5, 6.

The countdown had begun; 7 days to go, 6 days to go and so on. Only few days were left so we started spending more time with each other. Walks in the morning and evening had become common and we used to meet either at Chettinad canteen or in ice cream parlor. Those days were the best days of my life. Every time the clock struck 5 pm, I used to start from my house to meet her. It had become a habit in the last few days when we used to meet at ice cream parlor and order one kilo Ice cream tubs. We shared our lives with two spoons over those Ice cream tubs.

Time slipped quicker than the melting of those Ice creams. Sometimes Vinit, my roomie used to be with both of us, sharing the ice-cream with his spoon. Another day we thought to go to Mahaballipuram beach. So the trio had the best time on the beach before the last trip. Those fun moments at the beach remained were cherished forever.

Finally the day arrived- 19th June 2009, the last few hours of our stay in Chennai. We both were busy packing our stuff. It was a total of nine bags for her and three for me. We booked a cab for the railway station. That evening I went to her P.G. for the last time to collect the sim card and I handed both the sim cards to Abdul, who took them with a hope that with those lifelines of ours may become a backbone for his relationship, with a girl of his batch. Our train was scheduled for departure at 9:30pm. Around 6:30pm we started from Kelambakkam where we had stayed for four years. Friends who had decided to continue their stay in Chennai came to bid us goodbye. Aastha and I boarded the cab with the heap of bags. That day I was not aware of the fact that the journey would become the last journey together.

As we reached the station, Wasim was already there. Announcement was made and it was platform number four from where our train was about to start in the next half an hour. It's truly said you get attached with the place, people, food and culture once you stay for a long time in any place of the world. So leaving Chennai was painful for both of us, since we had spent the most beautiful moments of our life there.

Somehow we had managed to keep all those twelve bags on that extra seat which I had booked. I appreciated myself for the smart move; else managing the luggage would have been a big headache for us. But my thought was soon challenged by the ticket collector (T.C) when he enquired about my Dad on whose name the berth had been booked. I smartly answered that he was in different bogie, but somehow the TC could make out I was lying. He asked me to call my Dad while he started verifying other passengers' tickets.

I asked Wasim for his help as he was much smarter than me. He told me not to worry and offered to tackle the issue. By 11:00 pm after having *Biryani*, we all were about to sleep before the T.C came and enquired again about my Dad. I had to pretend saying that Dad had missed the train. My unreasonable convincing did not work out. However, Wasim was quick enough to talk to the T.C in his language and settled the matter with a fine of four hundred rupees. He went away without allotting that seat to somebody else.

Wasim and the rest of the five passengers soon slept in that coup. Aastha and I couched in a corner of the lower berth holding each others' hands. Unexpectedly we felt a jerk inside the bogie which was very unusual. Before we could make out anything, I heard a terrible sound and everything went dark in front of my eyes. The train had got de railed, something very hard was struck above my hand. My right hand was not holding anything then and I wasn't able to move. I screamed my lungs out but no one was there to respond since everyone was shouting and crying. Why did it happen to us? I could not move a bit and then what happened, I don't even remember.

How much time did I take to open my eyes, I don't know but I was not inside the train compartment anymore. I was in a hospital lying on a bed and I found my hand covered with crape bandage. I looked around to search for my *Babyjaan* and Wasim but there was no known face in that room. I was about to get up when a nurse came running towards me asking me not to move, since I had fractured my arm which had to be plastered. When I heard some people anticipating fifty deaths in that accident, I got cold feet. I wanted to shout, to run away from there and find out where was she and Wasim, but I could not move.

I was lost; I was dead. Not physically but emotionally. She could not leave me and go like this. I saw Wasim coming towards me. I was happy to see him. He was neither on the bed nor in the list of people who died in the accident. I noticed some first aid on his hand. He rushed to me and said that he had luckily escaped the accident as got thrown out of the bogie when the train de railed, since he was near to the emergency exit. Before he finished speaking, I asked him to search for Aastha. Wasim became a messenger for me running from one cabin to another and coming back to me to give the latest update. I was praying; praying hard to God to find her. GOD could not be so cruel to me. I needed her in my life, I needed her company in each step of my life, I needed her to have those ice-creams with me, I needed those fights, I needed her.

Wasim came running with Aastha's news. She was doing fine and survived minor injuries. She was in some other hospital. I sighed with relief with the piece of is information he brought to me. The nurse came and plastered my fractured arm. It took two hours till I was discharged from the hospital. Till that time Wasim was able to track our entire luggage except two bags, which were probably carrying her books. After I got discharged from the hospital, we rushed to the other hospital to see Aastha. I was amazed to see her was perfectly well, sitting at the entrance of the hospital. I got back my life, my smile, everything.

She came running towards us and hugged me. She cried and did not stop till I assured her that I was fine and alive. Finally we three returned to the station where we found that a special train had been arranged for the victims. I called my parents as well as hers, to assure them that we were safe and Wasim was with us. We were certainly lucky to have Wasim in that journey, else it would have been really tough to come out of this situation so easily.

The train journey began around 2:00 pm. She was there beside me nursing me and helping me to eat until I slept. A sudden thought struck my mind- Wish my both hands would have got fractured so that she could be with me showering more care and affection.

It was the morning of 21st June and I had to get down a few stations ahead of Aastha and Wasim. I was counting the hours and seconds and I wished we could have run away from there. I thought that in the next semester we would meet again. I wished there was one more year in the Engineering degree, but the fact was something else. I was still thinking about us being together; suddenly she interrupted me and said that I had reached my destination. Wasim helped me put my luggage at the platform as I reached my station. She was with me and got down at the platform to bid me good bye. She had tears in her eyes, but pretended as if nothing happened. We were in tears till the engines whistled and I said her goodbye for the last time, which was my last journey with her. My elder brother had come to take me home.

What made her to do so

☙

Back in our hometowns, life started as usual, only there were no early calls to wake me up, no more late night studies, and no more 24*7*365 phone calls. Life was changing gradually.

I was waiting for my offer letter, so was Aastha. It was her birthday, few days after that last journey. I wished her. Everything was sailing smooth. Our conversation started taking place through Internet. Our phone calls' frequency reduced since we were at home.

I thought to come to Delhi for higher studies preparation. Since both of my siblings were outside home, I decided to spend some time with my parents before I joined any institute. Against expectations, I got a job in my hometown in the position of Centre Manager and Soft Skill Trainer in an institute, which was nowhere related to my studies. Nonetheless, the new role excited me. Though, I was waiting desperately for my joining date in the MNC, where I was placed during my campus placement, I made the institute clear about my intentions. With their acceptance I joined them on 22nd July 2009.

Recession had truly taken a U-turn in many people's life (especially IT people) and I was also one of the victims among them.

Usually, Aastha and I used to chat with each on Facebook around 10:00 pm daily.

Should I thank God that there was no internet during our parent's time? Otherwise they would have got to know about our way of connecting to each other. Distance was killing both of us but we were happy that we are constantly there for each other at the end of the day and our hope was alive, that tomorrow would be better for us.

That night I remember our chat continued till 1:00 am. Since it was a video chat and we were seeing each other after two months, we were happy to feel romance in the air. Happily we both went to sleep without even smelling that the next day would be a day which would bring storm in our lives.

As usual, I went to office, took classes and was performing pretty well in my new role. Both, the management and students were quite impressed by my teaching approach. That day I took a motivational session for my students. Late night chatting was apparent in my sore eyes but somehow I managed to collect some videos and prepared PPT (Power Point) Presentation. I lectured a class of 25-30 students of different age groups. Some were even double my age. The moment I started with the lecture, I spoke nonstop. I felt a positive energy coming out of me when I was motivating that group of people who were my students at that moment. Their positive body language was enough to boost my energy level. I presented the video of Nick Vujicic- who had no arms, no legs, no worries, where I concluded, yes you can-trust yourself, if he can, why can't we?

The session was touching enough to bring tears to the eyes of few girls. I received a huge round of applause which made me feel proud of myself and the feeling that had quality in me, where my words could touch many hearts.

Days paced with this wonderful experience. I wanted to share my feelings with my parents back at home. I rushed in a hurry but there was something else waiting for me.

As I reached home, I saw my Mom talking to someone over the phone and passed on the phone to me when I entered the room.

It was *Babyjaan*'s mother at the other end. I never imagined about the question her mother asked me so early- "Do you love my daughter and want to marry her?"

I was shocked for a while and I thought to reply but checked myself, thinking "Is this the right time to disclose?"

I was considering my thoughts, when her Mom repeated the same question.

I came out of the room and said "Aunty I will speak to you when the right time comes, but we are very good friends as of now."

Even before I could finish my sentence her father (who was a very soft spoken man) interrupted me asking "Just say Yes or No."

How could I have replied in a word when it was a serious question concerned with my life! I could not figure out what to say. I was numb at that moment when I heard from her Mom that her daughter had told everything them about us. They concluded the conversation by saying, "It's all over and don't ever try to continue this. We have trusted you from last four years and this is what you gave us in return."

What made her disclose everything so early? Even the previous last night during our conversation over chat she did not mention anything. Why did she act like a fool? I heard a beep, the phone disconnected at the other end.

I came back to my room to face my parents. Some people in this world are blessed with supportive families and I am one among them. My father said "Don't worry; we will talk to you tomorrow. Have your dinner first and go to sleep."

The only thought I had in my mind was - what to do next. I was all alone. Whom to ask, what to do? I couldn't understand what made her reveal everything before time and why did she act so foolish. Next morning I took leave from work and dropped my parents to their office. I dint sleep last night thinking that the time had come to face it. I could not deny the fact any more.

I called her father and said, "Uncle, it's me and my reply is YES. We both love each other and want to marry."

He shouted at me, which I had expected. I tried to convince him. Her Mom took the phone from her father. I knew the fact that aunty was strict but never thought about the way she blamed me. I requested, begged, did whatever I could but failed to convince them. "Ok, if you love my daughter then leave everything and come to my house, we will allow you to marry her," said her father. Without thinking further, I asked him, "If, I come, will you allow me to marry her?" He could not say anything.

I have always cared, respected them in the same way I did for my parents. I was in great pain since I was not prepared to face her parent's disagreement so early, but life is not what we want it to be always. They finally said to me, "Our daughter doesn't want to have any relation with you, so you should not contact her anymore." They disconnected the call again.

I called them not once or twice, but many times. Nobody answered my call. I was ready to divulge the truth to my parents that evening. I didn't have anyone close to me that day, to ask for suggestion or a few words of support - I was in pain, my heart bled, I cried and shouted but no one heard me since I was all alone at home. Thanks to Vinit with whom I spoke over the phone and shared my soreness which helped me survive, at least at that moment.

That evening I waited for my parents to return home. I told them everything. My Dad used to be a short tempered person but that day he was exactly the opposite. He assured me that they are with me and decided to call her parents that very instant.

I was lucky and pleased to have my parents support, not many do so. He called Aastha's parents. It was ringing and my heart beats accelerated.

It was her father who picked the phone. My Dad introduced himself. I never expected her father to blame me. He made it clear that his daughter was never into this relation. My father wanted to speak to Aastha. "Can I talk to your daughter once? You have been talking to my son the last four years."

It took ten minutes for her to get on the phone, as I could hear that her Mom was coaxing her for refusal. She could not say anything except keeping mum for all the questions my father asked her about our relation. Silence changed into sobs and tears. Her mother snatched the phone and said to my Dad "Make sure, your son doesn't try to contact my daughter anymore." It was over but neither from my side nor from her. How could love be over?

I was not prepared nor wanted to listen to what was true, everything was scattered; my dream, our hopes and promises, that beautiful path of our life was now full of thorns. But I was ready to face it. That night my parents support gave me the strength to move ahead.

I continued with my job meanwhile and those 10pm chats, days were getting tough bit by bit. Phone calls' frequency reduced to minimum. It was August 2009, I received a mail from her and the subject was "Received the offer letter." I felt delighted to read the subject and thought she would be out of her family pressure. But once I read the complete mail, my heart was shattered. She wrote, "I was happy to see my offer letter, went to share it with Mom. But Mom wasn't happy at all. She tore my offer in front of me and I am not allowed to join anymore."

I was brokenhearted. The pieces of my broken heart got crushed with the mail. All those incidents flashed in front of me; how I took her to that campus interview, how she felt when she got selected. But all those efforts were washed away by her parents' decision, as if she had committed a crime; a crime to love someone.

She was forced to join a coaching institute in her home town for higher studies while I was still waiting for my offer letter of the MNC with a hope that may be tomorrow everything would be better.

Sometimes she missed 10pm chats and whenever she called me, her tears said the rest. Still I could not figure out what made her to do that so early? I never complained but we were victims of a crime. Finally, after waiting for quite long, I didn't receive my joining date. I then decided to go for higher studies preparation.

I resigned from my job on 15th May, 2010, after spending a good tenure and getting much respect and love from my students. On 30th May 2010, I accompanied my sister to Delhi who was returning to the Capital after spending seven days at home. I was on the verge of taking admission in some Institute again.

Hardly four days had passed when I was in the national capital that I received a call from someone for whom I had patiently waited all the while. It was my dream company's call who asked me to join on 7th June in Bangalore. Life had again made a joke of me; all uncertain things were written in my fate.

The time when I was waiting for the same, it was not for me and when I had decided to leave, it was calling me back. Had this offer been given to me few months ago, my life would have been different from what it was then. Should I join or leave, I was in doubt. I asked everyone my Dad, Mom, siblings, friends and *Babyjaan*. At last I decided to join that company which indeed was my life's first company where I started working. Getting into MNC is always a good feeling.

I had three days to leave for Bangalore while I was least prepared for the same. The next morning I travelled back from Delhi to my hometown Dhanbad and packed everything. I had to make my life's first flight journey from Kolkata to reach Bangalore on time. I was thrilled for my job and my journey, as it was the only ray of hope to prove my worth to someone .My elder brother was with me when I had to fly for Bangalore. I was requested to report on Monday morning in Bangalore. They had provided a fifteen day accommodation in a guest house for my family and me. That day I was not able to login to Facebook since I had to board the train to Kolkata at 11:00pm.I had a flight the next morning from there.

I started my journey from home again, many miles away but that time the reason was different. It was for a job which I had awaited from the last one year.

I received a text message from Aastha "*Dear apne aap pe hamesa vishwas rakhna,pehle se hi haar mat maan jana. Have a +ve attitude . M with u always. Hav a safe journey 2 day. Missing u....143. Kash aaj mai tumhare sath ja pati.*" (Please have faith in yourself, do not give up easily. Have a positive attitude. I am always with you. Have a safe journey. Missing you. I love you. I wish I could accompany you) the text message still lies in my phone inbox.

"Yes I will have positive attitude" I said to myself and continued my journey. I was at Netaji Subhas Chandra Bose airport at Dum-Dum at six in the morning. I was about to fly; high in the air with a hope that when I get back to Earth, those thorns would have been changed to flower petals in my path. It was Indigo flight and I got the window seat. The plane took off. The deafening sound of the takeoff was never heard by me before. I saw the airplane running fast on the runway and took a forty five degree vertical angel. I was in the air. High and higher, I was in middle of clouds.

I wish I could touch those clouds which appeared like snow balls. The sky was crystal blue flooded with cotton like clouds around. We landed in Chennai first as per the flight route. I saw many passengers getting down as they reached their destination but I was yet to reach. It was the same place which had given me everything, made me an Engineer, given me this job and so many other memories which would always remain in my heart. I called my Dean to share my happiness with her but she didn't attend my call. Later she sent me a text message saying that she was at somebody's funeral.

I opened my phone inbox and read *Babyjaan's* text message again

"m with u........................"

So Far but Yet So Close…

൙

After two months of stay in Bangalore I was transferred to Delhi. I was happy when I was flying on my way to Delhi from Bangalore because I was going to land in a city which was familiar to me, and my sweet sister was there.

10th August 2010, 1:00 pm. from temperature a temperature of fourteen degree Celsius at Bangalore to thirty four degree at Delhi was well felt by me and Abhishek Sharma, my mentor, my ideal from the first day I started my job at Bangalore.

I thought at least my 10:00 chats with Aastha would continue. I reached home and received a message from her "Don't forget me. Reply mat karna, cell is with Mom." (Don't forget me. Don't reply to this number, my mobile is with Mom) I thought to inform her that my journey was nice and I had reached safely but I couldn't do so. Not that I obeyed to her every time, but thought my small step shouldn't bring a worries or misunderstanding in her family. So even without taking off my shoes, I started writing a mail on my laptop.

I was alone that time, since my sister couldn't take leave that day due to her work pressure.

We were approximately fourteen hundred kilometers apart from each other. Yet I felt she stayed in the next lane.

I joined my office in Delhi and came to know that her parents had decided to make her study for Masters Degree after rejecting that offer. Since she and I had broken the trust of her parents, she was not allowed to go out of the city.

It was Friday. I remember I wanted to watch a newly released movie with my colleagues in the office but dropped the plan, since I was not feeling well. It was rainy season that time.

I opened my mailbox to see whether I received any mail from her or not. I saw three mails from her, each without a subject. The content was blank too.

I wondered the reason of sending three blank mails to me. Every other day I received her mails; same three mails with no subject or content. It became a regular affair for her to send three blank mails every day. I thought of calling her after three days of repeated instance. She was travelling in a bus. I tried her number again. She replied with a text massage "Please don't call before I give you a missed call, at home now."

I could judge how much she was under pressure and worried that if her Mom got to know about our association, she might stop that by some way or other. Whether I was a wrong guy or was I at fault, I wondered. For reasons unknown, till date, her parents have shown disagreement about our relation. She was caught between meeting her parents' expectation and listening to her own heart. It was getting tough for her which I could very well understand.

It was during September, I received a mail from her. The subject was mentioned in double code "Nearly more than a year-haven't seen you." It was actually more than a year; the last time we were together was that last bus journey we made together in June 2009.

I don't know if I should term it madness or love for her that made me reply- "No more waiting, see you soon." I had only one thing going in my mind that a distance of fourteen hundred kilometers would never stop me to meet her.

And one fine morning, I decided to be with her. Distance

could stop me, and no distance was big enough to make me away from her. I stuffed a bag with two sets of dresses, my diary, pen and a small gift- a teddy with the words "I missed you so much" for her.

I booked my ticket which was waitlisted at number five. And as always my parents and sister extended their full support to me. My sister came to drop me to the station at seven in the morning. She hugged me and said "Take care and come back soon."

Train started its journey and so did I. I managed to get a seat next to a gentleman whose first question was "Don't you have a confirmed Ticket?" I convinced him, "Let the TC come. I will manage something."

But soon I had to search a new seat again, since by that time the gentleman was ready to sleep.

I kept shuffling between bogies till I got the T.C by evening 7:00 pm when I was at Mugal-Sarai station. He did not assure me a seat yet said would try. I wondered how to spend the entire night since it would be around next morning till I reached my destination. I counted the number of hours left to meet her 12, 11, 10, 9, 8.I was meeting her after one year and three months.

It was 10:00 pm. The train was crossing Bihar. The passengers were about to sleep. The last seat where I had made my place on, the lady next to me said "*Beta aap jagah dekh lo, mujhe ab sona hai.*" (Son, please find a new place for yourself. I have to sleep now)

With my bag over my shoulder, I stood in front of the train's entry door. I am sure you must have felt the same at some point in time of your life that an upcoming happiness makes you forget everything. I thought of lying down on the floor though in the mid-way results in blockage of way for other passengers.

I locked the door from inside and managed to sit in front of it. I spread a newspaper which I spread on the floor. It saved my trouser.

I observed all passengers had slept by that time and the full coach was dark except for the light above my head. I tried to find its switch but lights near washrooms are meant to be switched on the whole night.

And then it was me, my pen and diary where I could write down some lines.

Dastaan

Tere bin zindagi adhoori si hai
Ye raahein, yeh raatein sab sooni si hai..
Le jaaengi ye raahein na jaane kaha,
Kisko fikar kisko pata

Chootha tha jab, tera mera sath
Banti hui bigdi thi baat..
Likhni jo chahi wo humne dastaan,
Reh gai adhoori bas choote kuch nishan.

Wo Dastaan... Wo dastaan

Un beete lamho ki,
Tanha si raato ki,
Un bigdi baton ki,
Dastaan....

Un bheegi yaadon ki,
Bhikhre Jazbaaton ki,

Ankahi si baton ki
Dastaan…

Toote hue sapno ki,
Ruthe hue apno ki,
Dil ke armano ki,
Dastaan…

(courstey- G.P.Singh)

Somebody kicked me. I opened my eyes and found myself sitting on the floor near the gate, with my open diary and pen.

It was CRPF. I realized it was dusk already and I was about to reach.

6 am, I was in her city without even knowing where we could meet, would I be able to meet her or not. But still I was there. I went straight to a hotel.

It's true sometimes someone plays such a vital role in our life which we never expect from them. That instant, I received a call from one of her roommates of our college time, Shanti. Even before listening to her, I asked her to convey Aastha that I was in her city and call me.

May be it was Shanti's effort or our luck; I received a call from her. We planned to meet at Sai- Baba temple near the bus-stand of her city around 11:30 am.

I took a shower; reached there around 10:30 am much before the time. I couldn't wait longer to see her.

I believe that one doesn't have to go the temple in search of God, as God is everywhere. But that day was an exception like the time I used to visit temples with my Mom.

The clock ticked and I patiently waited.

I saw many faces, but no face was the one for whom I was waiting.

I kept waiting till twelve noon. It had been more than one and a half hours but she was nowhere in sight. But I knew she would come.

Suddenly I saw her. I saw a girl approaching towards me with books in her hand. I saw her beautiful face lost somewhere; the pain she had been through, the tears which she had shed, were apparent on her face.

It was my *Babyjaan* in front of me. Was that a dream? I touched her. She was really in front of me. After so many ups and downs we were together.

We boarded an auto from there and went to a restaurant. During that journey till restaurant I could only ask her about her college and studies.

While we sat in the restaurant, she said she had three hours, since she had to college to meet me.

I had to live my life in three hours, ask her so many questions, and tell her so many things. Would three hours be enough?

We began with our conversation. She seemed different to me then, a bit afraid a bit tensed and much tired. I just asked her "Are you happy?" She broke into tears. I hugged her and told her that we would face it and surely win one day.

Those tears had lot of pain within. An over ambitious girl, who was born to reach the zenith, got a job, got a good result but had to leave everything for a crime she committed, she had loved someone and it was me.

I shunned my questions within myself and decided not to ask her anything to aggravate her pain. I was living my life; spending three hours together appeared to me as three seconds. That was the maximum time my *Babyjaan* would stay with me.

Sometimes tears are also meant for happiness. My tears gave way to smiles. I smiled because I was with her.

I thought of cracking jokes to change the grave mood, as we both had turned very emotional then. I started telling her about my job.

Her frame of mind changed. I could at least make her smile. I could see that happiness on her face. I thought to give her surprise with the teddy I had brought for her. While talking to her I took that teddy in my hand and hid it behind myself. I was waited for the right moment. Meanwhile we ordered lunch. The food was about to be laid on the table when suddenly I saw someone push through the gate of the restaurant.

God knows if he didn't want her to smile, or was he against our happiness.

It was her Dad, right in front of us. I dint get words in my mouth and was about to say, "Uncle, I was about to come" I was interrupted by her Dad. He said something harsh, but that was not for me, it was meant for her. "You repeated the mistake," and suddenly that smile which we were sharing was washed away. Her father gripped her hand and took her away from me. She walked away looking at me, with welled up eyes.

Lunch was served on the table. I was alone- all alone, the gift I had brought for her was with me and my lips were murmuring- *Babyjaan*. I was in pain.

My journey, my effort to meet her, and probably that meeting was over. I called her father several times but he did not respond.

I asked the waiter to pack the food and wanted to head straight away to her home and speak to her parents. But again I stopped thinking-"What would I say, how can I marry her now, my two elder siblings were unmarried, my step may hurt her parents and mine too." I stopped, took the packet of food in my hand which had left with no taste for me, and while I was walking on the street, I saw the boy who was pulling my trousers asking for money. I handed him the plastic bag that carried the food which we ordered few minutes ago.

My heart ached. My eyes full of tears but I was not able to cry. What was stopping me to do so was her father's statement one year back "Don't be a Coward." I was strong but not so much that I could not understand that heaviness in my heart.

I went back to the hotel, picked up my bag and moved out to start my journey for returning to Delhi.

My phone inbox blinked again, It was her message "Take care, miss u…met with a small accident but don't worry it was just a small one...m fine"

Sometimes we get the urge to do many things but life doesn't allow us, or we don't want our life to do so. I checked if I could get a train back to Delhi. "You can buy a general ticket and get it converted from the T.C on the way," suggested the ticket-counter person for the train which was about to enter the platform.

The train arrived. I began with my journey. There was only one difference between the last journey and the journey that day; last day my heart was full of happiness to meet her and that day it was full but of a pain, of leaving her in that world where I don't know when we would meet again.

I in the train on my way back to Delhi.

I opened my diary and saw the lines...

Toote hue sapno ki,
Ruthe hue apno ki,
Dil ke armaano ki,
Dastan………….

Never said, nor wanted-
!!STILL WE ARE APART!!

 C3

That incomplete journey was fresh in my heart. I was back to the city. With course of time, things moved on; going to the office in the morning at nine, returning by six in the evening. I was getting used to the routine. What was changing was those 10:00 pm chatting, sometimes that started around 11:00 sometimes 12:00 or sometimes never. Yet we were connected to each other through social sites. We could hardly call each other in a gap of fortnight. But we were moving ahead with a hope.

Suddenly she didn't come online one day nor had I receive any call from her in the next ten days. Since my hands were tied, I asked one of our common friends to call her. She conveyed to me that nobody was responding to the calls .Few days later I received a mail from her quoting "Dad had to be admitted" without any content in the mail body. I guessed that the tension which had caused because of our relationship must have the reason for his ill health.

I was right. When I received a call from her two days later, her Dad had been admitted after a severe heart attack –she told me. I wished I could stand by her during that tough time of her and her family "But how could I, since I was the reason behind this mishap." I said to myself. Being the only child of parents is sometimes good and sometime bad too, I realized that day.

It took approximately fifteen days for them to discharge her father. As her father was the only earning person in her family, it did them affect them economically too. I know she was going through the toughest time of her life, and our relation was the reason for it.

I was paralyzed, thought to do so many things, but could not turn them into reality. After many "Ifs & buts" I called her Mom that evening to ask about uncle's health and any support if they required.

I knew she would shout at me, but ignoring the fact I did make a call. That day it made me realize that how much she hated me. As I called her, she asked me very calmly-"How did you get to know about my husband's condition, who told you?"

I tried to beat around the bush and said, "I got to know from your neighbor, who is in touch with me." I didn't drag Aastha's name else her Mom would have broken her, instead of breaking that cell phone. The last words I heard were, "Will you please leave me and my family alone?" Her words pinched me, quite alike breaking or throwing something.

I regretted to have made that call to her. I cursed myself "What made me call her, why did I show my care and concern to them. I can't even talk to her now."

A month passed away, no phone call no mails from Aastha.

It was November 2010 when I received a mail from her after two months quoting –"Why you did that, why did you call my mother, thanks for everything." Who was wrong – I, Aastha, her parents, our love or the situation? Who so ever I blame, the victims were my *Babyjaan* and I.

I was moving on with a faint hope that someday will bring happiness in our lives and it would be better than before. The 10:00 pm chats did not happen anymore. It had been more than four months that I received any communication from her side; no phone call, no message, no mail. Every day I survived seeking God's blessings. My friends suggested me many ideas; like to take her away from there, or court marriage, and so on. But I was not convinced with any idea although I happy to get back all seven friends in my life.

I finally decided to take a step which I thought would make my *Babyjaan* and me together forever.

I discussed with my parents. Though my both siblings were yet to get married, my society was a hindrance. I neglected the social obligations. My only concern was to get blessings and support from my family. No parents in the world would like to see their child take such decision but as I said few lucky children get their support always and I was one among them. I left Delhi again this time with something different in my mind. Finally I had decided to take the extreme step.

I boarded the train from New Delhi railway station, but this time with a confirmed ticket and even my return ticket was booked in Rajdhani Express(12313) coach no B9 seat number 31 and 32, side upper and side lower berths.

I was prepared and even aware of the consequence of this but I was left with no option. I reached her city again ,this time did not even book any hotel since our return train was on the same day .I was sure that she would come with me, because nothing was impure from her side, neither the care, nor love and tears.

I knew her address. I took an auto and went to her house. It was on the first floor. While climbing the stairs, I felt once that I din't want to hurt her parents this way but I had to live my life. I reached in front of door and knocked it. Once twice and then…

(Charrrrrrrrrr sound of opening of the door)

The door opened and a lady stood in front of me asking me whom was I searching for. I was shocked. Neither it was she, nor was it her Mom. The lady was not even a relative since I had seen all her relatives' pictures and videos during college time, then who was she? I was mum for few minutes and then asked, "There used to be a family- one daughter and her parents where are they?"

She was a little surprised by my question. She replied "We are here from the last four years."

"But I was here on 10th June 2006, during my training," I replied. "How is that possible?"

She replied, "Beta, its 2011, five years from then, sorry you ask someone else" and closed the door. "How it could be possible. She didn't mention about it anytime, but why did she hide this," I said to myself while coming down.

I tried her number- "the number you are trying to call doesn't exist" was the response I received.

I called her mother's number. Same reply, "Please check the number you are trying to call."

I tried her father's number; it was ringing "Tring tring"

I was happy to hear the tone at least. It was a harsh and blunt voice from the other end. I asked quoting her Dad's name. The disconnected the call calling it a wrong number.

I tried the number again and told him, "Look Sir, I spoke to uncle on this number during 2009. Are you sure it's a wrong number?"

He replied, "Arre bhaiya, its 2011; now people change their numbers in one minute and you are surprised to see a change after two years." But how come the same number was assigned to someone else in so less time. I recollected I had never spoken to her father on his number after college days.

I was in the middle of the road praying to God "Please allow me to meet her once, just once. I want to see her just once. I will go away from her life, but please God, please allow me to meet her once." I searched everywhere, tried every corner to get information about her, but no one was able to provide me any. I was left with one hope but to visit her college where she was doing her Masters from.

I took an auto and went straight to her college. As soon as I reached her college I jumped out of her auto. The auto driver shouted "Bhaiya paise to de do." (Pay the fare) I came back, paid him the fare and started walking towards her college main gate.

I knew her department and few faculties name as she used to discuss with me sometimes about her college.

I saw her department room and went inside to meet her professor.

She was around fifty five years of age. I introduced myself and enquired about Aastha. Her reply shocked me- "She has left the college some 6 months ago," and added, "And where is she staying we don't know."

She used to be quite tensed, much worried. That's the information I got about her when I asked few of her batch mates, but no-one was able to give me her address, or contact number since no one was in touch with her.

I felt an acute pain in my chest, which no one could see nor can I explain but that pain increased to its peak. My eyes did not get tears. I went to a cyber café nearby to send her a mail but was shocked to receive a non delivery message that the recipient's id was wrong. I tried once, twice, thrice and continued till those two drop of tears rolled down my cheek. She was not on my Facebook page anymore. It's true I had not checked Facebook from the last four months but did open my mailbox daily to check any mail.

Was I too late to reach? Was she forced to marry someone else, or was she no more in the world or she decided to be away from me always? Questions haunting me till I boarded my train. I had to come back since I didn't die physically nor did I want to lose as she told me through message "Pehle se he haar mat jana," .Till today I believe she never said, nor I wanted –still we are apart...................

And I keep on saying I Am Still Committed..

As Hopes are yet to die.

⠶

That long stretch yet empty road
That full moon yet dark night
That one hope yet a lie
That one day you will come back
I wanted to stop you for a while
To show you my love and walk beside you in every mile
I don't know what made you take such decision
I don't know why you didn't hear my confession
I don't know what my mistake was
But it's tough living without you after that day dear
Now it passes so many years
I didn't see you nor did I hear
I am sure somewhere you still think about me
Though you will never express nor will you say it to me
I have started to accept this reality
But don't know why I can't erase it from my memory
Each day while returning back home
You come to my mind and yes I do miss
Each moment you were with me
Each word you have said to me
Each way you have shown me
How we have lived life for each-other
And again in that long stretch yet empty road

I find a full moon yet dark night
This makes alive that one hope yet a lie
And I dream that one day you will come back

Message from Pashupati Nath Singh (MP Dhanbad)

℘

I am extremely glad and proud to see a boy of Dhanbad who is professionally a Software Engineer has turned into an Author.

It's our wish to see this novel turned into a National Best seller and remains in the heart of the reader forever. Our good wishes are with Soumitro and his debut novel "I Am Still Committed"

To my dear Readers

☙

*I*don't know how much the story have connected you or how you *felt. I had written this journey of my life not just to get myself recognized as an Author but this work of mine was only to increase the happiness and reducing the pain I am carrying in my heart.*

My friends still use to tell me to move ahead in my life, yes I have moved ahead now in other things .With the way I have been able to utilize myself in every possible work, I have involved myself in my job, my writing and my weekends are meant for Kids of Prayas.

"Because life is not what you lose rather what you gain my losing something."

If I can add any value to your life, it will be an honor for me to get in touch with you
@
https://www.facebook.com/Soumitro28

And if you feel you can share this novel with others you can do by visiting
https://www.facebook.com/pages/I-Am-Still-Committed-Soumitro-Chatterjee/155541167896577

Soumitro Chatterjee

www.ingramcontent.com/pod-product-compliance
Lightning Source LLC
Chambersburg PA
CBHW060120260626
47160CB00005B/1952